Kate Hewitt

THE LONE WOLFE

TORONTO NEW YORK LONDON
AMSTERDAM PARIS SYDNEY HAMBURG
STOCKHOLM ATHENS TOKYO MILAN MADRID
PRAGUE WARSAW BUDAPEST AUCKLAND

Recycling programs
for this product may
not exist in your area.

ISBN-13: 978-0-373-13048-1

THE LONE WOLFE

First North American Publication 2012

Copyright © 2011 by Harlequin Books S.A.

Special thanks and acknowledgment are given to Kate Hewitt for
her contribution to The Notorious Wolfes series

www.Harlequin.com

Printed in U.S.A.

All about the author...
Kate Hewitt

KATE HEWITT discovered her first Harlequin® romance novel on a trip to England when she was thirteen, and she's continued to read them ever since. She wrote her first story at the age of five, simply because her older brother had written one and she thought she could do it, too. That story was one sentence long—fortunately, they've become a bit more detailed as she's grown older.

She studied drama in college and shortly after graduation moved to New York City to pursue a career in theater. This was derailed by something far better—meeting the man of her dreams, who happened also to be her older brother's childhood friend. Ten days after their wedding they moved to England, where Kate worked a variety of different jobs—drama teacher, editorial assistant, youth worker, secretary and, finally, mother.

When her oldest daughter was one year old, Kate sold her first short story to a British magazine. Since then she has sold many stories and serials, but writing romance remains her first love—of course!

Besides writing, she enjoys reading, traveling and learning to knit—it's an ongoing process and she's made a lot of scarves. After living in England for six years, she now resides in Connecticut with her husband, her three young children and, possibly one day, a dog.

Kate loves to hear from readers. You can contact her through her website, www.kate-hewitt.com.

Other titles by Kate Hewitt available in ebook:

Harlequin Presents®

2978—THE UNDOING OF DE LUCA
3008—THE MATCHMAKER BRIDE*
3015—THE SANDOVAL BABY
        (Anthology title: **The Secret Baby Scandal**)

*The Powerful and the Pure

To my fellow writers in this continuity: thanks for making it such a fun journey!

CHAPTER ONE

WOLFE MANOR was no more than a darkened hulk in the distance when Mollie Parker's cab pulled up to its gates.

'Where to now, luv?' the driver called over his shoulder. 'The gates are locked.'

'They are?' Mollie struggled to a straighter position. She'd been slumped against her bags, the fatigue from her flight catching up with her, making her content to doze gently in the warm fug of the taxi. 'Strange, they haven't been locked in ages.' She shrugged, too tired to consider the conundrum now. Perhaps some local youths had been wreaking havoc up at the old manor house yet again, throwing stones at the remaining windows or breaking in for a lark or a dare. The police might have needed to take matters a step further than they usually did. 'Never mind,' Mollie told the cabbie. She reached into her handbag for a couple of notes. 'You can just drop me here. I'll walk the rest of the way.'

The cabbie looked sceptical; not a single light twinkled in the distance. Still, he shrugged and accepted the money Mollie handed him before helping her take her two battered cases out of the cab.

'You sure, luv?' he asked, and Mollie smiled.

'Yes, my cottage is over there.' She pointed to the forbiddingly tall hedge that ran alongside the gates. 'Don't worry. I could find the way with my eyes closed.' She'd walked the route between the gardener's cottage and the manor many times, when Annabelle had been living there. Her friend had rarely left the estate, and Mollie, the gardener's tearaway daughter, had been one of her only friends.

But now Annabelle was long gone, along with her many brothers; Jacob, the oldest, had started the exodus when he'd turned his back on his family at only eighteen years old. He'd left the manor house to slowly moulder and ruin without a single thought of who might age along with it.

Mollie shrugged these thoughts away. She was only thinking this way because she was tired; the flight from Rome had been delayed several hours. Yet as the cab drove off and she was left alone in the dark without even the moon to cheer her or light her way, she realised it was more than mere fatigue that was making her rake up old memories, old feelings.

After six months travelling through Europe, six months she'd put aside, selfishly, just for herself and her own pleasure, coming home was hard. Coming home was lonely. There was nobody—had been nobody for so long—living at Wolfe Manor except her.

And she wouldn't be here very long, Mollie told herself firmly. She'd pack up the last of her father's things and find a place in the village or perhaps even the nearby market town, somewhere small and clean and bright, without memories or regrets. She thought of the notebook in her case with all of her new landscaping ideas, a lifetime of energy and thought just waiting to be given wings. Roots. And she would make it happen. Soon.

She straightened the smart, tailored jacket she'd bought at a market in Rome, and tugged a bit self-consciously on the skinny jeans she wasn't used to wearing. Her knee-length boots of soft Italian leather still felt new and strange; she generally wore wellies. The clothes, along with the notebook of ideas, were all part of her new life. Her new self. Mollie Parker was looking forward.

Smiling with newfound determination, dragging her cases behind her, Mollie made her way along the high stone wall that separated the manor from the rest of the world. The high hedge met the wall at a right angle, and although it was dense and prickly Mollie knew every inch of it; she knew every acre of the Wolfe estate, even if none of it belonged to her. She'd only been in the house a handful of times—it had always been an unhappy place, and Annabelle had preferred the cluttered warmth of the cottage—but the land she knew like her hand, or her heart.

The land felt like it was hers.

Halfway down the hedge Mollie found the opening that had always been her secret. No one, not even the boys from the village who snuck up here on dares, knew about this hidden little entrance. She slipped through the gap in the hedge, and headed towards home.

The gardener's cottage was hidden behind yet another high hedge, so that it was completely separate from the manor house. The small garden surrounding it was cloaked in darkness, yet Mollie wondered just how overgrown and weedy it had become. She'd left in midwinter, when everything had been barren and stark, rimed in frozen mud, but from the heady fragrance of roses perfuming the air she knew the garden—her father's garden—had sprung to life once more.

A lump, unbidden, rose to her throat. Even in the velvety darkness she could picture her father bent over his beloved roses, trowel in hand, gazing blankly around him. The world had shifted and changed and moved on and Henry Parker had stayed in the crumbling confines of his own mind until the very end…seven months ago.

Mollie swallowed past that treacherous lump and reached for her key. Starting over, she reminded herself. New plans, new life.

Inside, the cottage smelled musty and unused; it was the

smell of loneliness. She should have asked a friend from the village to open the windows, Mollie thought with a sigh, but communication with anyone had been difficult. Now she reached for the light switch and flipped it on.

Nothing happened.

Mollie blinked in the darkness, wondering if the bulb had gone out. Had she left the lights on six months ago by accident? Yet as she gazed through the gloom she realised there was not one sign of electric life in the cottage. The clock on the stove was ominously blank, the refrigerator wasn't humming in its familiar, laboured way; everything was still, silent, dark.

The electricity had been turned off.

Mollie groaned aloud. Had she forgotten to pay a bill? She must have, even though she'd paid in advance in preparation for her trip. Perhaps there had been a mixup. Something must have happened, some annoying piece of bureaucratic red tape that left her fumbling in the darkness when all she wanted to do was have a cup of tea and go to bed.

Sighing, Mollie kicked her suitcases away from the door and reached for the torch she kept in the old pine dresser. She found it easily, and flicking the switch, gave a grateful sigh of relief as the narrow beam of light cut a swath through the darkness.

Yet her sigh ended on something sadder as she shone the torch around her home. Everything was as it should be: the table tucked into the corner, the sagging sofa, the old range and ancient refrigerator. Her father's boots were still caked in mud, lined up by the door. The sight was so familiar, so dear, so *right*, that she couldn't imagine them not being there, and yet...

All around her the house was silent. Empty. At that moment Mollie was conscious of how alone she was, alone on the Wolfe estate, with the huge manor house vacant and violated a few hundred metres away, the cottage empty save her. Alone in the world, as the only child of parents who had both died.

Alone.

Jacob Wolfe couldn't sleep. Again. He was used to this, welcomed insomnia because at least it was better than dreaming. Dreams were one of the few things he couldn't control. They came unbidden, seeped into his sleeping mind and poisoned it with memories. At least his active, conscious brain was under his own authority.

He left his bedroom, left the manor house, not wanting to dwell in the rooms that held so much pain and regret. No, he corrected himself, refusing to shy away from the truth even in the privacy of his own mind. Not wanting—not *able*. Living at Wolfe Manor for the past six months as he oversaw its renovation and sale had been the most harrowing test of his own endurance.

And now, as sleep eluded him and memories threatened to claim him once more, he feared he was failing.

He stalked past his siblings' bedrooms, empty and abandoned, forcing himself to walk down the curving staircase that was one of Wolfe Manor's showpieces, past the study where nineteen years ago he'd made the decision to leave the manor, leave his family, leave himself.

Except you couldn't run away from your very self. You could only control it.

Outside the air was fresher, soft with night, and he took a few deep cleansing breaths as he reached for the torch in the pocket of his jeans. The memories of the manor still echoed in his mind: *Here is where my brother cried himself to sleep. Here is where I nearly hit my sister. Here is where I killed my father.*

'Stop.' Jacob said the single word aloud, cold and final. It was a warning to himself. In the nineteen years since he'd left Wolfe Manor, he'd learned control over both his body and brain. The body had been far easier—a test of physical strength and endurance, laughably simple compared to the mind. Control over the sly mind with its seductive whispers and cruel taunts was difficult, torturous, and no more so than here, where his old demons—his old self—rose up and howled at him to escape once again.

The dreams were the worst, for he was vulnerable in sleep. For years he'd kept the old nightmare at bay and it had ceased—almost—to hurt him. Yet since he'd returned to Wolfe Manor the nightmare had returned in full force, and even worse than that. Even in its aftershocks he could feel his clenched fist, hear the echo of trembling, wild laughter.

He took another breath and stilled his body, stilled his mind. The thoughts retreated and the memories crouched, silent and waiting, in the corners of his heart. Jacob flicked on the torch and began to walk.

He knew most of the gardens now, for he'd taken to walking through them at night. He doubted he'd ever cover every corner of the vast Wolfe estate, but the neat paths, admittedly now overgrown, soothed him; the simple order of flowers, shrubs and trees calmed him. He walked.

The air cooled his heated skin, and his mind blanked, at least for a little while. He thought of nothing. He walked with purpose, as if he were going somewhere, yet in reality he had no destination.

Renovating the manor to sell it? You're just running away again.

His brother Jack's scathing condemnation echoed emptily within him. Jack was still angry with him for leaving in the first place; Jacob had expected that. Understood that. He'd already seen the flickers of disappointment and pain in all of his siblings' eyes during their various reunions, even though they'd forgiven him. He'd reconciled with everyone except Jack, and while he'd steeled himself to accept the pain he'd caused, he hadn't realised how much it would *hurt*.

How the regret and guilt he'd pushed far, far down would rise up and threaten to consume him, so he couldn't think of anything else, feel anything else. He'd abandoned his brothers and sister, and even though he'd accepted the fact and even the need of it long ago, the reality of the hurt and confusion in their faces near crippled him again with the old guilt.

Where was his precious control now?

Jacob stopped, for something danced in the corner of his vision. His senses prickled to awareness, and he turned his head.

Light.

Light was flickering through the trees, dancing amidst the shadows. Had teenagers broken in again and started something in the woods? Fires, Jacob knew from his long experience on building sites, could easily get out of control.

He strode through the copse of birches that divided the once-ordered, once-organised garden from a separate untamed wilderness. Determination drove him; he had a purpose now.

He stopped short when he emerged through the trees into another, smaller garden, a place he'd never been before. In the centre of the garden a little stone cottage was huddled like something out of a fairy tale, complete with a miniature turret. And the fire was coming from inside, illuminating the windowpanes with its flickering light.

Jacob had never even known about the existence of this cottage, but he sure as hell knew it was on his property. And so was the trespasser inside it. The dream he'd just escaped still flickered at the edges of his mind and fuelled the anger that made him march towards the cottage.

He stopped in front of a stable door whose top half was made of pretty mullioned glass, and in one brutal, effective movement, kicked it open.

He heard the scream first, one short, controlled shriek before it stopped, and in the gloom of the cottage's small front room he blinked, his vision focusing slowly. A woman stood by the fireplace hearth, half bent over as she tended to its flickering flames. The light from the fire danced over her hair, turning it the same colour as the flames.

She straightened now, a log still held in her hands. A weapon.

Of course, as a weapon it posed no threat. With nearly twenty years' training in the martial arts, Jacob knew he could disarm the trespasser in a matter of seconds. But he wouldn't hurt her. He wouldn't hurt anyone ever again.

His gaze flicked over her appearance; she was not what he'd expected. Auburn curls cascaded down her back in an untamed riot, and her skin was as pale as milk. She wore some stylish, trendy outfit, utterly unsuitable for a life in the country.

What was she doing here?

And then her eyes, already dilated with shock, widened even further and the log dropped from her hands.

'Jacob?'

Mollie hadn't recognised Jacob Wolfe when he'd burst through her front door like a madman from a horror film. She'd only screamed once, the sound abruptly cut off as truth dawned, and with it shock. Jacob Wolfe—the lord of Wolfe Manor—had returned. He was older, of course, and bigger, his body sinewy and yet with the muscles of a man. Even in her shocked state Mollie took in the way the faded grey T-shirt and old jeans clung to his powerful frame. His hair was dark and rumpled and just a little long, his eyes dark too, black and cold. He held a torch in his hand, and its beam was pointed directly at her.

It was impossible. He was gone, maybe dead, disappeared in one afternoon, leaving seven siblings broken-hearted. He hadn't been seen or even heard from in twenty years.

And yet now he was here. *Here*, and as Mollie stared at

him, she felt a confusing welter of emotions: surprise, relief, even a strange joy. And then, suddenly, a sharp needle of anger stabbed her. She'd seen how Jacob's departure had affected his siblings; from afar she'd witnessed their own sorrows and struggles. And she'd struggled herself; in the long, lonely years since Jacob had left, Mollie had wondered if the crumbling of the manor and the wild ruin of the garden had speeded her father's own descent into dementia. She'd often imagined the seductive *what-ifs*...what if Jacob had stayed, if all the Wolfes had stayed, if the manor had remained loved and lived in, and the gardens as well...?

Yet now it was too late. Now her father was dead, the Wolfes all gone, the manor a falling-down wreck. Now Jacob was back, and Mollie wasn't sure she was glad to see him.

Standing there now, staring at him, at his coldly composed face, so handsome, so blank, she felt the bitterness rush back, filling the empty spaces in her heart and mind.

'You know me?' His words were careful, controlled and completely without emotion.

Mollie let out a short, abrupt laugh. 'Yes, I know you. And you know me, although you obviously don't remember. I know I was always easily forgotten.' Even that rankled. She'd watched the Wolfe siblings play together, seen them tramp off to London to go to their fancy department store, and in some desperate corner of her childish heart she'd been jealous. Their lives had been torn apart by unhappiness and despair—who didn't know that? Yet at least they'd always had one another...until Jacob had left.

Jacob's eyes narrowed, and his gaze swept around the dismal clutter of the cottage. Her bags still lay in a heap by the door, and Mollie was conscious of all the things she hadn't thrown out before she'd left, because she hadn't been ready to. Her father's pipe and tobacco pouch on the mantel, his coat hanging on the door. Even her father's post was stacked on the table, a jumble of flyers and bills and letters that no one would ever answer.

'You're the gardener's girl.'

Indignation rose up inside her; it tasted sour in her mouth. 'His name was Henry Parker.'

Jacob turned to face her again. His eyes were cold and grey and so very shrewd. 'Was?'

'He died seven months ago,' Mollie replied stiffly.

'I'm sorry.' Mollie nodded jerkily in acceptance and Jacob's glance flicked to the suitcases by the door. 'You just returned…?'

'I've been in Italy.' Mollie realised how it sounded; her father died and she swanned off to Italy? She refused to explain herself. Jacob Wolfe could think what he liked. She would not make excuses. He did not deserve explanations.

'I see.' And Mollie knew just how much he thought he saw. 'And you returned to the cottage because…?' It wasn't so much a question as an accusation.

'Because this is my home,' Mollie replied. 'And has been since I was born. You may have run out on Wolfe Manor, but that doesn't mean the rest of us did.'

Jacob tensed, his body stilling, and Mollie felt the sense of latent anger like a shiver through the room. Then he relaxed and arched one eyebrow, the expression eloquently contemptuous. 'Wolfe Manor is your home?' he inquired with a dangerous softness.

Fury raced through Mollie's veins and burst in her heart. 'Yes, it is, and always has been,' she snapped. 'Even if you never thought of it that way. But don't worry,' she continued before Jacob could say something scathing in reply, 'I'm not staying long. I just came back to pack up my things and then I'll be on my way.'

Jacob folded his arms. 'Very well.' His glance took in the small, cluttered cottage. 'That shouldn't take too long.'

Mollie's mouth dropped open in indignant outrage as she

realised what he was implying. 'You want me to leave *to-night*?'

'I'm not completely heartless, despite what you seem to think,' Jacob said coolly. 'You can stay the night.'

Mollie swallowed. 'And then?'

'This is private property, Miss Parker.'

Staring at him now, his eyes so black and pitiless, his expression utterly unyielding, every grudge and hurt she'd held against Jacob Wolfe crowded her mind and burst from her lips.

'Oh, I see,' she managed, choking a little on the words. 'You don't have enough space up at the manor. You need this little cottage as well.'

'It's private property,' Jacob repeated. His expression didn't flicker.

'It was my *home*,' Mollie threw at him. Her voice shook, but only a little bit. 'And my father's home. He died in the bed upstairs—' She stopped the words, the memory, because she didn't want Jacob sharing it. She certainly didn't want him to pity her. Besides her four years doing a degree in horticulture, this had been the only home she'd ever known. It churned in her gut and burned in her heart that Jacob Wolfe was going to throw her out without so much as a flicker of regret or apology, especially considering how her father had given his very life for the wretched Wolfe family.

Yet how she could protest? She'd been living here rent-free for years, and Jacob was right, it *was* private property. It had never been hers. She'd grown up with that knowledge heavy in her heart; she could certainly live with it now. She swallowed, lifted her chin.

'Fine. I need a little time to go through my father's things, but then the cottage is all yours.' It hurt to say it, to act so nonchalant, yet Mollie forced herself to meet Jacob's hard gaze. He was just speeding up her plans by a few days or weeks, that was all.

Jacob continued to look at her, his expression considering. His gaze swept over the cluttered room, seeming to rest on various telling items: her father's boots, his pipe, her suitcase. 'You have somewhere to go,' he said, more of a statement than a question.

'I want to let a place in the village,' Mollie said. It was not precisely a confirmation, because she did not in fact have any arrangements made. Jacob must have realised this, for his gaze sharpened as it rested on her; it felt like a razor.

'And what will you do with yourself? Do you have a job?'

Mollie bit her lip. 'I run a gardening business,' she admitted reluctantly. 'But I'm hoping to expand into landscaping and garden design.'

'Oh?' His eyebrows arched as he took in this information. Then he nodded once, briskly, as if coming to a decision. 'Well, in that case perhaps we can come to a mutually beneficial arrangement.'

Mollie stared at him in bewilderment. She could not imagine how anything between them could be mutually beneficial. 'I don't—'

'If you'd like to stay in the cottage,' Jacob cut across her, 'you can earn your bed and board. You'll work for me.'

CHAPTER TWO

HE REMEMBERED her now. She'd followed him—all of them—when they were younger, gap-toothed and tousle-haired, peeking at him and his brothers and sister from the tangled limbs of a tree or behind a hedge. She'd barely registered on his radar; he'd had seven siblings to protect and provide for. The gardener's daughter had been completely outside his authority or interest.

More recently he'd seen her image plastered over the walls of Annabelle's room. His sister must have taken Mollie Parker's photograph a hundred times. And he could see why: with her pale skin and tumbling, auburn hair, she possessed a Titian beauty that seemed almost otherworldly, especially considering how he'd stumbled upon her in this enchanted little place. It had taken a moment to connect this flashily dressed interloper with the laughing, graceful girl on his sister's bedroom walls, but now Jacob recognised the tumbling curls and creamy skin. She was beautiful, stylish, and he had no idea why she would be in this place.

On his property.

Why had Mollie Parker gone off to Italy the moment her father had died? Why had she returned? And what was he going to do with her now? The look of uncertainty and fear in those soft, pansy-brown eyes annoyed him, because he didn't want to deal with it. He didn't want to deal with the outraged Miss Mollie Parker. He had enough to worry about,

managing the renovation and sale of Wolfe Manor, and at-
tempting, as best as he could, to repair his fractured family.
Concerning himself with a stranger's well-being was not on
his agenda. He didn't need the feeling those proud yet plead-
ing eyes stirred in him: something between curiosity and
compassion, something real and alive. He hadn't felt anything like that in…years. Nineteen years.

And he wasn't about to feel it again.

He watched her gaze steal to the boots by the door. Her father's boots, he suspected. Seven months on, she would still
be grieving. He felt an uncomfortable jab in his conscience
as he realised he could have been more sensitive; the unex-
pectedness of her presence, and her vulnerability, had caught
him on the raw. For a single moment, with her fancy clothes
and her trip to Italy, he'd assumed the worst. It had not taken
long to realise his mistake, but then, it never did.

Still, Jacob didn't want to have to deal with her. Think
of her. Be affected by her. And yet something in her eyes
reached out to him, spoke to him, and despite his misgivings
and even his fear, he answered that silent call.

He would help her and at the same time assuage his own
conscience. He'd given her the commission of a lifetime.

'Work for you?' Mollie repeated incredulously. She felt another sharp stab of anger. 'My father worked for you for
fifty years, and for the past fifteen he didn't even get a pay
cheque.'

Jacob stilled. Mollie realised she'd surprised him. She
wondered if he'd thought of her father at all in the past nineteen years. He obviously hadn't concerned himself for a
moment with her. 'I'm not talking about your father,' he replied after a moment. 'You are the one in need of a place to
stay, and I happen to be in need of—'

'I won't be your maid. Or your cook. Or—'

'Landscape designer?' Jacob finished softly. Mollie

almost thought she heard laughter lurking in his voice. She must have imagined it, she decided, for Jacob's expression was as coldly foreboding as ever.

'Landscape designer?' she repeated, testing the words. 'You can't—'

'You told me you were planning to start a garden design business. And I happen to need someone to landscape the estate's gardens.'

Mollie blinked, realisation dawning. 'That's—that's a huge job,' she replied faintly.

Jacob lifted one shoulder in an indifferent shrug. 'So?'

'But…a job like that…' She paused, her heart beating with sudden, frantic desperation. She didn't want to disqualify herself for such an amazing opportunity, but her own conscience required that she explain to Jacob the absurdity of what he was suggesting. 'An offer like that should go to a much more experienced landscaper,' she said quietly. 'It's a huge commission.'

'I know,' Jacob replied drily. 'And you do too, apparently, yet you're throwing it away with both hands.'

'Why are you asking me?' Mollie persisted. She could not fathom why Jacob Wolfe, after so many years away, would now offer her such a huge commission, and without even reviewing a CV or reference! Looking into his cold, hard eyes, he did not seem like a man to be moved by pity. So what did he want?

'Because you're here,' Jacob replied, his voice edged with impatience, 'and I need a landscape designer. I also need to turn around this place quickly, and I don't have time to trawl through endless CVs of hopeful gardeners.'

'Turn around?' Mollie repeated. 'You're *selling* Wolfe Manor?'

Jacob's mouth curved in a smile that was both bitter and mocking; there was nothing warm or funny or even human about it. Yet somehow the sight of that cruel little smile made

Mollie feel only sad. No one should smile like that. She couldn't even imagine the feelings that lay behind it, inside him. 'Too much space for just one person,' he said softly.

Heat flooded her face as she recalled the words she'd thrown at him. *You don't have enough space up at the manor.* Well, she'd been angry. And she still didn't know what Jacob Wolfe was about. Was he doing her a favour? Was this really *pity*? The thought made her want to throw the commission right back in his face, even if it was the stupidest thing she'd ever do in her life. 'Still—'

'It's late,' Jacob cut her off. 'And frankly, when I went for a relaxing midnight stroll, intruders were not on my mind. If you're so concerned about your own abilities, you can show me some initial designs tomorrow.' He turned to the door he'd so unceremoniously kicked in just moments before. 'And if you don't, you can start packing tonight.'

Mollie watched him leave, his tall frame swallowed up by the darkness, and she sagged against the fireplace hearth. She glanced at the cosy glow she'd created moments before; all that was left was smoking ash.

Her mind spun in dizzying circles. It was all too much to process: coming back home, seeing her father's things, meeting Jacob Wolfe again and now this commission.... The past and the present had come together with an almighty crash.

Sighing wearily, Mollie pushed her tumbled thoughts to the back of her already disordered mind and, after closing the door—Jacob had as good as vanished into the night—she retrieved her torch and headed upstairs. It didn't matter that there was no light, or water, or even food in the non-working refrigerator. There were sheets on the bed, only a little musty and damp, and she was exhausted.

Kicking off her Italian leather boots, shedding the clothes that she'd never truly felt comfortable in, Mollie tumbled into bed and then gratefully, blissfully, into sleep.

* * *

She woke to bright summer sunlight streaming in through the diamond-paned windows of her bedroom. She blinked, groggily, yet within seconds it all came crashing back: the cottage, the job, *Jacob*.

She leaned back against her pillow and closed her eyes, yet the image of Jacob danced before her closed lids. He'd looked so much older, so much more rugged and weary somehow. What had he been doing for the past nineteen years? Why had he come back now? Was he in need of a little cash? Was that why he was selling Wolfe Manor?

Mollie told herself not to rush to conclusions. She'd thrown enough accusations at Jacob last night. She'd tried and judged him years ago, even when Annabelle, who as his younger sister had far more cause, had not. Annabelle, when she'd talked of her family, which had been rarely, had always seemed willing to forgive Jacob, to assume the best.

Last night Mollie had assumed the worst.

Had Annabelle seen Jacob? Did she know he was back? Did any of the Wolfe siblings know? So many questions. So few answers. And, Mollie acknowledged, sighing, none of it really concerned her anyway. She'd always danced on the farthest fringes of the Wolfe family, watching as Jacob and Lucas took their younger siblings out for a picnic, or played hide-and-seek amidst the vast grounds. No one had ever known she existed, until Jacob had left and Annabelle, scarred both inside and out, had retreated to the manor, refusing to show her face in public again. Then Mollie had been a friend, because she didn't have any others.

But the other Wolfes—Jacob included—had never so much as looked in her direction. And they'd never considered what it would mean to her or her father to let Wolfe Manor fall into such desperate disrepair.

Shrugging these thoughts away, Mollie got out of bed. Now was the time to think of the future, not the past. Jacob Wolfe wanted some landscaping designs by the end of today,

and she'd give them to him. Mollie didn't know when she'd
decided to accept the commission; but when she'd awakened
in the morning she realised she already knew. This was too
important to throw away in a moment of pique or pride, and
there was something redemptive, something *right*, about restoring Wolfe Manor's gardens to their former glory. She
wasn't doing it for Jacob, or even for herself. She was doing
it for her dad.

She pulled on her old gardening clothes—jeans and a
worn button-down shirt of her father's—and tied her hair
up in a careless knot. No point impressing Jacob Wolfe with
her stylish new clothes. He hadn't looked impressed last
night, and the effort would be useless considering without
water she couldn't even have a shower or so much as brush
her teeth. Armed with her notebook and a couple of pencils,
Mollie put on her wellies and headed outside.

It was one of those freshly minted days of early summer,
when the trees, impossibly green, glinted with sunlight, and
every furled flower was spangled with diamond dewdrops.
Mollie took several deep breaths, filling her lungs with the
fresh, damp morning air. She felt a rush of feelings: happiness, homesickness, sorrow and hope. Excitement too, as she
left the cottage's little garden for the unkempt acres beyond.

Over the years, as her father's condition had worsened and
he'd been unable to tend to his duties—few as they were—
on the estate, Mollie had taken over what she could. She'd
kept up the small garden surrounding the cottage, enabling
her father to exist in his own little make-believe world where
the manor was lived in and the gardens were glorious, the
roses in full bloom even in the middle of winter. Meanwhile,
all around them, the estate gardens had fallen into ruin along
with the house.

Now she walked down a cracked stone path, the once-
pristine flower beds choked with weeds. Sighing, she noticed
the trees in desperate need of pruning; for many, pruning

wouldn't even help. There was enough dead wood to keep the manor stocked with logs for its fires for a year.

The manor's rose garden was a particular disappointment. It had once been the pride of the estate—and her father—designed nearly five hundred years ago, laid out in an octagonal shape with a different variety of rose in each section. Henry Parker had tended each of these beds with love and care, so often absorbed in nurturing the rare hybrids that bloomed there.

Mollie's heart fell as she saw what had befallen her father's precious plants: as she stooped to inspect one, she saw the telltale yellow mottling on the leaves that signalled the mosaic virus. Once a rose bush had the infection, there was little to be done, and most of the bushes in the garden looked to have contracted it.

She straightened, her heart heavy. So much loss. So much waste. Yet there were still pockets of hope and growth amidst all the decay and disease: the acacia borders were bursting with shrub roses and peonies; the wildflower meadow was a sea of colour; the wisteria climbed all over the kitchen garden's stone walls, spreading its violet, vibrant blooms.

She found a bench tucked away underneath a lilac bush in the Children's Garden. Her father had known all the names of the formally landscaped plots, and he'd told them to Mollie. The Rose Garden, the Children's Garden, the Water Garden, the Bluebell Wood. Like chapters in a book of fairy tales. And she'd loved them all.

Now she laid her notebook on her knees and took out a pencil, intending to jot down some ideas, but in truth she didn't know where to begin. All she could see in her mind's eye was the weeds and waste…and her father's lined face, concern etching his faded features as he worried about whether Master William, long dead, would be disappointed to see the beds hadn't been weeded.

Perhaps landscaping the Wolfe estate gardens was too big

a job for her. She had so little practice, so little experience, and the thought of ploughing under even an inch of her father's beloved flowers and trees made her heart ache. Yet clearly this couldn't just be a patch-up job; the Rose Garden alone would have to be nearly completely replaced.

Leaning her head back against the stone wall, Mollie closed her eyes and let the sun warm her face, the sweet scent of lilacs drifting on the breeze. She felt incredibly weary, both emotionally and physically. Too tired even to think. She didn't know how long she sat there, her mind blank, her eyes closed, but when she heard the dark, mocking tones that could belong to only one man her eyes flew open and she nearly jumped from the bench.

'Hard at work, I see.'

Jacob Wolfe stood in the entrance to the garden, his hands in the pockets of his trousers. He wore a steel-grey business suit, his cobalt tie the only splash of colour. He looked coolly remote and arrogantly self-assured as he arched an eyebrow in sardonic amusement.

'You can't rush the creative process,' Mollie replied a bit tartly, although her mouth curled up in a smile anyway. It was rather ridiculous, having Jacob catching her practically taking a nap. She straightened, aware that unruly wisps were falling from her untidy bun and her clothes were sloppy and old. Jacob, on the other hand, looked cool and crisp and rather amazing.

'I wouldn't dare,' he murmured, and Mollie's smile widened. Were they having a civil conversation? Or were they—unbelievably—*flirting*? 'I've just been walking through the gardens to assess the damage,' she explained, her tone a little stilted. Her heart was beating just a little too hard.

'So you'll take the job.'

Now she actually laughed. 'I suppose I should have said that first.'

'Never mind. I'm glad you got right to it.'

Jacob looked so grave that Mollie's tone turned stilted again. 'Thank you. It's an amazing opportunity.'

'You're welcome.' He glanced around the enclosed garden. 'I don't think I've ever been here before.'

'It's the Children's Garden.'

'Is it?' He continued looking around, as if he'd find a stray child hiding underneath one of the lilac bushes like some kind of fairy or elf.

'I always thought there should be something more child-like about it,' Mollie admitted ruefully. 'Like toys.'

Jacob nodded in the direction of the fountain that reigned as the centre piece of the small space. 'I suppose that's where it gets its name from.'

'You're quick,' Mollie said with a little laugh. 'It took me years to suss that.' She glanced at the fountain of three cherubic youths, each one reaching for a ball that had just rolled out of reach. It was dry and empty now, the basin filled with dead leaves.

'Did you come here as a child?' Jacob asked, and Mollie nodded.

'My dad took me everywhere. I know these gardens like my own hand, or I did once.' She gave a small, sad laugh. 'To tell you the truth, it's been years since I've walked through them properly.' She lapsed into silence, and when Jacob did not respond, she cleared her throat and attempted to change the subject, at least somewhat. 'When are you hoping to sell the manor?' she asked, a bit diffidently, for she wasn't even sure how she felt about the manor being sold. It had been Jacob Wolfe's home, but it had encompassed hers as well.

'By the end of the summer. I can't stay here longer than that.'

'Why not?' She couldn't keep the curiosity from her voice; she had no idea what Jacob did or had been doing with his life. Did he have a job? A home? A *wife*?

Mollie didn't know why that last thought had popped into

her head, or why it left her with a strange, restless sense of discontent. She shrugged the feeling away.

'I have obligations,' Jacob replied flatly. He obviously wasn't going to say any more. 'Why don't you come back to the house? We can discuss whatever you need to begin your landscaping, and agree on terms.'

'All right,' Mollie agreed. She glanced down at the blank page of her notebook, and wondered just how much they would have to discuss. If Jacob wanted to hear her ideas, she didn't have any yet. The sun was getting warmer as she followed Jacob back to the manor, and while she felt her own hair curl and frizz and sweat break out along her shoulders and back, she noticed a bit resentfully that Jacob looked utterly immaculate, as unruffled as stone, as cold as marble. Nothing affected him. Nothing touched him.

Was that why he'd been able to walk away? To leave his brothers and sister, his entire family, without so much as a backwards glance?

And what of his father? Mollie felt a chilly ripple of remembrance. She'd only been eight, but she remembered the furore of the press, the gossip of the village, when Jacob had been arrested for the murder of his father. In the end he'd been let off; everyone agreed it was self-defence. And William Wolfe had been a brute in any case. The entire village had rallied around Jacob, and there had never been any doubt that he'd been simply protecting himself and his sister. Yet walking behind Jacob, Mollie could not keep herself from thinking: *he killed a man.*

Almost as if he guessed the nature of her thoughts, Jacob paused on the threshold of the house, turning around to give her the flicker of a cool smile. 'I realise that as we're the only two living on the estate, you might feel, at times, vulnerable. I want to assure you that you are completely safe with me.'

Mollie flushed with shame at the nature of her own thoughts. They were utterly unworthy of either her or Jacob.

She might be a bit angry at him, and bitter about all the lost years, but she was not at all afraid. In fact, there was something almost *comforting* about Jacob's steady presence, and she realised that despite the fact he'd broken into her cottage last night, she did feel safe with him. Secure. The thought surprised her, even as she acknowledged the rightness of it.

'Thank you for that reassurance,' she said a bit pertly, desperate to lighten the mood even a little bit, 'but it's really not necessary. I know I'm safe.'

Something flickered in Jacob's eyes, and his mouth twitched. She might feel safe with him, but Mollie knew she had no idea what he thought. Felt. He gave a brief nod and led the way inside.

Outside, the manor was covered in scaffolding, and inside, Mollie could see how much work was being done. The floor was draped with drop cloths, and ladders lay propped against different walls; nearly all the furniture was covered in dust sheets. From somewhere in the distance she heard the steady rhythm of a hammer.

'You're hard at work, I see,' she said, parroting his words back at him, and was rewarded with a tiny smile, one corner of his mouth flicking gently upwards. It was, Mollie realised, the first time he'd smiled since she'd seen him, and it did something strange to her insides; she felt as if she'd just gulped too much fizzy soda and was filled with bubbles.

Then he turned away from her and she was left flat.

Uh-oh. She didn't want to be feeling like that, didn't want to have any kind of ephemeral, effervescent reaction to Jacob Wolfe. She knew what that kind of feeling signified, what it meant.

Attraction.

Desire.

No way. Jacob Wolfe was not a man to dally with. Yes, he might exude a steady presence, but that control had a ruthless, unyielding core. He'd walked away from his family and responsibilities without a single explanation, had remained silent for nineteen years, letting his siblings fear and think the worst. She could not, would not, allow herself to be attracted to him even for an instant, even if he was incredibly good-looking, even if she'd always thought he had the same perfectly sculpted look as the prince in her old book of fairy tales, except with dark hair and no smile.

Even when he was younger he hadn't smiled much—at least, not that she could remember. He'd always seemed serious, preoccupied, as if the weight of the world rested on those boyish shoulders. Of all the Wolfe children, Jacob had fascinated her the most. Something in his eyes, in his beautiful, unsmiling face, had called out to her. Not that he'd ever noticed.

He turned back to her again, and she took in the clean, strong lines of his cheek and jaw. She smelled his aftershave, something understated and woodsy.

'Right this way,' Jacob murmured, and led her into what seemed to be the only room that remained untouched by the renovations. William Wolfe's study.

Mollie gazed around the oak-panelled room with its huge partners' desk and deep leather chairs and a memory flooded over with her such sudden, merciless detail that she felt dizzy. Dizzy and sick.

She'd been four or five years old, brought here by her father, holding his hand. The office had smelled funny; Mollie remembered it now as stale cigarette smoke and the pungent fumes of alcohol. Of course she hadn't recognised those scents as a child.

Jacob must have seen or perhaps just sensed her involuntary recoil as she entered the room, for he turned around with a wry, mocking smile and said, 'I don't particularly like this room either.'

'Why do you use it, then?' Mollie asked. Her voice sounded strange and scratchy.

Her father had been asking for money, she remembered. He was a proud man, and even at her young age Mollie had known he didn't like to do it.

I haven't been paid in six months, sir.

William Wolfe had been impatient, bored, scornful. He'd refused at first, and when Henry Parker had doggedly continued, his head lowered in respect, he'd thrown several notes at him and stalked from the room. Still holding her hand, Henry had bent to pick them up. Mollie had seen the sheen of tears in his eyes and known something was terribly wrong. She'd completely forgotten the episode until now, when it came back with the smells and the sights and the churning sense of fear and uncertainty.

She looked at Jacob now; he was gazing around the room with a dispassionate air of assessment. 'It's good for me,' he said at last, and Mollie wondered what that meant. She decided not to ask.

She moved into the room, stepping gingerly across the thick, faded Turkish carpet, her notebook clasped to her chest as if she were a timid schoolgirl. The memory still reverberated through her, made her realise—a little bit—what Jacob and his siblings had endured from their father. She'd experienced only a moment of it; they'd had a lifetime. Annabelle had never really spoke of her father to Mollie, never wanted to mention the terrible night that had given her the scar she was so self-conscious about.

Mollie was starting to realise now just how much she didn't know.

'Here.' Jacob held out a folded piece of paper. 'This is yours, I believe.' Mollie took it automatically, although she had no idea what it could possibly be. Nothing of hers had ever been at the manor. 'I had the water and electricity turned back on at the cottage,' Jacob continued. 'So you should be comfortable there for however long the landscaping takes.'

Mollie barely heard what he'd said. She had opened the paper he'd given her, and now gaped at it in soundless shock. It was a cheque. For five hundred thousand pounds.

'What...?' Her mind spun. She could barely get her head around all those noughts.

'Back pay,' Jacob explained briefly. 'For your father.'

Ten years of back pay. Her fingers clenched on the paper. 'You don't—'

'Whatever you may think of me, I'm not a thief.'

Mollie swallowed. How did Jacob know what she thought of him? At that moment, she didn't even know herself. And she was beginning to wonder if the assumptions and judgements she'd unconsciously made over the years about Jacob Wolfe were true at all. The thought filled her with an uneasy curiosity.

'This is more than he would have earned,' she finally said. 'A lot more.'

Jacob shrugged. 'With interest.'

'That's not—'

'It's standard business practice.' He cut her off, his voice edged with impatience. 'Trust me, I can afford it. Now shall we discuss the landscaping?'

What had Jacob been doing, Mollie wondered, that made half a million pounds a negligible amount of money? Stiffly she sat on the edge of the chair in front of the desk. She slipped the cheque into her pocket; she still didn't know if she ever would cash it.

'Thank you,' she said, awkwardly, because how did you thank someone for giving you a fortune, especially when it seemed to matter so little to him?

Jacob shrugged her gratitude aside. 'So.' He folded his hands on the desk and levelled her with one dark look. His eyes, Mollie thought, were endlessly black. No silver or gold glints, no warmth or light. Just black. 'You mentioned there was damage. Besides the obvious?'

'It looks like a virus has claimed most of the bushes in the Rose Garden. There are a lot of dead trees that need to be cleared and cut, and of course all the stonework and masonry need to be repointed.' Jacob nodded, clearly expecting her to continue. 'I don't want to take away from the beauty of the original design,' Mollie said firmly. 'The gardens' designs are at least five hundred years old in some places. So whatever landscaping I do, I'd like to maintain the integrity of the original work.'

'Of course.'

'Like you're doing with the house,' she added. 'Aren't you?'

There was a tiny pause. 'Of course,' he said again. 'The house is a historic monument. The last thing I want to do is modernise it needlessly.'

'Who is overseeing the renovations?'

'I am.'

'I mean, what company. Did you hire an architect?'

Another tiny pause. 'J Design.'

Mollie sat back, impressed. 'They're quite good, aren't they?'

Jacob gave her the faintest of smiles. 'So I've heard.'

She glanced around the room; even with the windows thrown open to the fresh summer day, she thought she could still catch the stale whiff of cigarette smoke, the reek of old alcohol. Or was that just her imagination? She felt claustrophobic, as if the house and its memories were pressing in on her, squeezing the very breath and life out of her. She could only imagine how Jacob felt. He had so many more memories here than she did. 'When are you hoping to put the manor on the market?'

Jacob's face tightened, his mouth thinning to a hard line. 'As soon as possible.'

'You won't miss it?' Mollie asked impulsively. She didn't know what made her ask the question; perhaps it was the force of her own memories, or maybe the way Jacob looked so hard, so unfeeling. Yet he'd cared enough to give her her father's back pay and then some. Or was that just out of guilt or perhaps pity? Did the man feel anything at all? Looking at his impassive face, she could hardly credit him with any deep emotion. 'It was your home,' she said quietly. 'Whatever happened here.'

'And it's time for it to be someone else's home,' Jacob replied coolly. Mollie could tell she'd pushed too far, asked too much. He rose from the desk, clearly expecting her to rise as well. 'Feel free to order whatever you need to begin the landscaping work. You can send the bills to me.'

The thought was incredible. The greatest commission she'd probably ever receive, with carte blanche to do as she liked. It was like a dream. A fantasy. Yet she still felt uneasy, uncertain…and no more so than when she looked into Jacob's dark eyes. It was like looking into a deep pit, Mollie thought. An endless well of…sorrow. The word popped into her mind, as unexpected as a bubble—the bubbles she'd felt earlier. Perhaps sorrow was an emotion he felt.

'Thank you,' she finally said. 'You're putting an awful lot of trust in me.'

Jacob's face twisted for no more than a second, and something like pain flashed in his eyes. Then his expression ironed out, as blank and implacable as ever. 'Then earn it,' he replied brusquely. 'Starting now.' He walked out of the study, leaving Mollie no choice but to follow.

CHAPTER THREE

MOLLIE threw herself into the work. She wanted to, and it was easier than dealing with the other demands of her life... packing up her father's things, or thinking about her own future, or wondering about Jacob Wolfe.

She spent an inordinate amount of time doing the latter. She wanted to ask him where he'd been, what he'd done, why he'd come back. She never got the chance. In the week she'd been back at Wolfe Manor, she'd hardly seen Jacob since she'd walked out of his study.

Emails from Annabelle didn't clarify the situation too much. Now that the electricity was working in the cottage, she'd finally managed to check her email. There were at least a dozen from Annabelle, detailing Jacob's arrival at the manor, warning Mollie that he didn't know she was at the cottage. Wryly Mollie wished she'd thought to check her email while in Italy. Access had been limited, and frankly she'd been happy to escape the world and all of its demands for a little while.

It felt good to work hard with her hands all day, to get sweaty and dirty and covered in mud. She came back to the cottage every night to shower and fall into bed, too tired even to dream.

And yet still, in her spare and unguarded moments, her thoughts returned to Jacob again and again. She wanted to ask him questions. She wanted to know what he'd been doing all these years, and what he was doing now. She wanted to see him again. Just to get some clarity, Mollie told herself. And some closure. Explanations that would justify why he'd left everyone in such a lurch. Nothing more.

Except even as she told herself that was all, she knew it wasn't. She thought of the darkness of his eyes, the crisp scent of his aftershave, and knew she wanted to see him again, full stop.

A week after Jacob gave her the commission Mollie was still removing all the weeds and dead wood in preparation to actually begin the landscaping and give the garden new life. She'd hired a tree surgeon from the neighbouring village to come to the manor and cut some of the larger trees down, yet when he didn't arrive and the hours ticked on, annoyance gave way to alarm.

She rung the man's mobile, only to have him explain without too much apology, 'Sorry, but I called the manor to check on some details, and was told to cancel.'

'What…?' Mollie exclaimed in an outraged squeak. 'Who told you that?'

'I dunno…someone there who picks up the phone, at any rate. Sorry.'

And Mollie knew who that would be. There were only two of them here after all. And she wasn't supposed to feel *vulnerable*. Well, she didn't. She felt bloody cross. She'd wasted a whole day waiting for someone who had no intention of coming, and Jacob had not even had the courtesy to inform her he'd cancelled her arrangements. She was operating on a tight schedule already, and she certainly didn't need his interference.

After rearranging a time with the tree surgeon, she stalked to the manor. If Jacob Wolfe was going to interfere with her job, she wanted to know why. And she'd also tell him to butt out. She looked forward to the sense of vindication. Yet when she knocked on the manor's front doors so hard her knuckles ached she received no response. She peeked in the windows and rattled the doorknob, uselessly, for the house was locked up. Above her the sky was heavy and dank, and she felt as if its weight were pressing on her. It looked ready to pour, and she was too annoyed and out of sorts to head back to the gardens in this weather.

Mollie decided to return to the cottage. She'd take the opportunity to start sorting through her father's things, something she'd put off for far too long already. As she headed down the twisting path through the woods, the first fat drops began to fall.

An hour later, freshly showered and dressed in comfortable trackie bottoms and a T-shirt, Mollie started through her father's things. She'd picked the least emotional of his possessions: boxes of old bills and paperwork that had never managed to be filed. Yet even these held their own poignancy; Mollie gazed at her father's crabbed handwriting on one of the papers. He'd been jotting notes about a new rose hybrid on the back of a warning that the electricity would be turned off if a payment wasn't made. She thought of the crumpled notes William Wolfe had thrown at her father, and how he'd picked them up. Her heart twisted inside her.

As if on cue, the lights flickered and then went out, and Mollie was once again left in darkness. She sat there in disbelief, the notice still in her hand. Then anger—unreasonable, unrelenting fury—took over. First the tree surgeon was cancelled. Now the electricity was turned off—again! If Jacob Wolfe had changed his mind about having her stay here, he could have just said.

Without even thinking about what she was doing, Mollie yanked on her wellies. She reached for her torch and her parka and slammed out into the night.

It had been pouring all afternoon, and the deluge from the heavens had not stopped. Despite her rain gear, Mollie was soaked in seconds. She didn't care. Righteous indignation spurred her onwards, stalking through the trees, all the way up to the manor house steps. She knocked on the door as hard as she could, but the sound was lost in the wind and the rain. She knocked again, and again, sensing, *knowing*, that Jacob was home, despite the darkened windows. And even if he wasn't, she refused to slink back to her servant quarters yet again. She wouldn't be stopped by a closed door. Not this time. With a satisfying loud thwack, Mollie kicked the door.

'Ow!' The door swung open, and hobbling on one foot, she practically fell into Jacob's arms.

'Are you all right?' Unruffled as ever, he righted her, his hands running down her arms, pausing on her waist and then examining her calves and feet. Even in her outrage and pain, Mollie registered a curious tingle as he touched her, so lightly, so impersonally, yet with obvious concern, his fingers deft and sure. 'Did you break a bone?' She thought she detected the tiniest trace of amusement in his voice, yet she had to be mistaken. His touch and his expression were both impersonal, emotionless.

'No, I just stubbed my toe,' she snapped. She stepped away from him and those light, capable hands. He reached behind her to close the door.

'Is something the matter?' Jacob inquired, and Mollie let out a sharp laugh.

'I'll say something's the matter! Why did you cancel the tree surgeon I'd arranged? He's booked solid through June, and I only got the appointment by calling in a favour. And if you had to cancel, you could have at least told me—'

'I'm sorry,' Jacob replied coolly. 'I'm afraid it was an oversight. I was in London for the day on business and I had all my calls routed through my office. My assistant must have cancelled the appointment.'

'Oh.' Mollie didn't know what to say after that. She found herself imagining the assistant, some sexy, polished city girl in red lipstick and kitten heels. 'Well, why did you turn off the electricity?' she finally demanded, blustering once again. 'If you'd changed your mind about me, you could just—'

'*I* turned off the electricity?' Now Jacob looked truly amused. 'I'm afraid I don't have that much authority. The wind and the waves do not obey me.' He glanced around the foyer, and suddenly Mollie saw just how dark the manor was. She noticed the torch in Jacob's hand, and understood, far too late, that the electricity must be off in the manor as well.

It was a *storm*, for heaven's sake. Even though she was shivering with cold, her cheeks reddened. She was a complete idiot, coming in here full of fury, and for what? Jacob had a reason for everything.

'Oh.' She shifted, and muddy water leaked out of a ripped seam in her boot. She stared at the spreading stain on the rug, and saw that Jacob was looking at it too. 'I'm sorry,' she mumbled, feeling both foolish and stupid. 'I jumped to some awful conclusions.'

'So it would appear.' Jacob let the silence tick on rather uncomfortably as he gazed at her for a moment, and Mollie suffered through it. Perhaps this would be her penance. 'Well, I can hardly send you out in that storm the way you are now,' he said, sounding resigned. 'Fortunately the plumbing has already been repaired. Why don't you dry off upstairs? Have a bath if you like. You can change into something of Annabelle's.'

Mollie's eyes widened as an array of images cartwheeled across her brain. 'I couldn't—'

'Why not?' Jacob challenged blandly. 'Surely there's nothing waiting for you back at your cottage? I was just making myself some dinner. I only got back from London an hour ago. You are free to join me.'

Free, not welcome. Mollie was under no illusion that Jacob actually wanted her company. She was an obligation; perhaps she always had been. Perhaps that was what lay behind the cheque she still hadn't cashed, as well as the commission he'd given her. Just his wretched sense of duty.

Yet he obviously hadn't felt any sense of duty to his family; why should he feel it for her? Confused by her own thoughts, Mollie found herself nodding.

'All right, I will. Thank you,' she said, and heard the challenge in her voice. Maybe now was the time for the clarity and closure she wanted. Maybe now she'd get some answers.

'Good. You know the way?'

Mollie nodded again, and Jacob turned from here. 'Take all the time you need. I'll meet you in the kitchen when you're done. Don't forget your torch.'

Without waiting for her to respond, he walked away, swallowed by the darkness.

As he stalked down the hall back to the kitchen, Jacob wondered why he'd just invited Mollie Parker to share his dinner. He wished he hadn't. He didn't want any company, and certainly not hers. She gazed at him with an unsettling mix of judgement and compassion, and he needed neither. He refused to explain himself to her, yet he couldn't stand the thought of her jumping to more asinine conclusions.

She'd assumed he'd turned off the electricity again, just as she assumed he'd walked out on his family to follow his own selfish desires. He saw the condemnation and contempt in her eyes, had heard it in her voice that first night.

You may have run out on Wolfe Manor, but that doesn't mean the rest of us did.

Jacob closed his mind to the memory. There was no point in thinking of it, of her, because he had enough people to apologise to and enough sins to atone for without adding Mollie Parker to the list. He'd give her dinner and send her on her way.

Yet even as he made that resolution, another thought, treacherous and sly, slipped into his mind.

You invited her here because you want to see her. Want to talk to her. You want her.

He'd avoided her this past week for too many reasons, on too many levels. Yet now her auburn curls and milky skin flashed across his mind; he could almost *smell* her, damp earth and lilac, and his gut clenched with a helpless spasm of lust. He was annoyed—and angry—with himself for indulging in such pointless, useless thoughts. Desires.

He'd had enough meaningless affairs, engaged in enough no-strings sex, to know when a woman was off-limits. And Mollie Parker, with her pansy eyes and tremulous smile and fearsome fury, had strings all over her. There was no way Jacob would ever get involved with her beyond the barest of business details.

The day he'd left Wolfe Manor, he'd made a vow to himself never to hurt anyone again, never to allow himself the opportunity. It was a vow he intended to keep; he knew his own weakness all too well. And *anyone* included Mollie Parker.

It was strange to be in Annabelle's room. Mollie had only been here a few times, and then not for years, and she now saw that the walls were covered in photographs: artful pictures of a rainy windowpane, a bowl of lilies. And her. Many of the photos were of her; she'd forgotten how Annabelle had asked her to pose. She'd been her first reluctant model. Mollie stepped closer, shining her torch over the photos, now faded and curling at the corners. In half the photos she was posing rather unwillingly, looking both silly and pained. The other half were candids.

Annabelle had caught so many emotions on her face. It was strange, to see yourself so unguarded. There was a photo of her at age thirteen, gangly, awkward, a look of naked longing in her eyes as she stared off into the distance, caught in the snare of her own daydream. Her at sixteen, dressed up for a date—an unusual occurrence—looking proudly pretty. Nineteen, her arm loped around her father's shoulders. He was smiling, but there was a vague look in his eyes that Mollie hadn't seen then. The descent to dementia, unbeknownst to her, had already started.

She turned away from the photos, feeling shaken and exposed. Jacob must have seen all these pictures. He'd glimpsed these moments of her life that she hadn't even been aware of, and it left her feeling vulnerable and even a little angry. Annabelle should have taken the photos down. Jacob should have.

Pushing the thoughts away, she turned towards the en suite bathroom. She'd intended just to dry off with a towel, but when she saw the huge marble whirlpool tub she gave in to the decadent desire for a long, hot soak. The cottage's old claw-footed tub and sparing amount of hot water made it especially tempting. She turned the taps on full and within moments was sinking beneath the hot, fragrant bubbles, all thoughts of the photographs and everything they revealed far from her mind.

Half an hour later, swathed in a thick terry towel, a little embarrassed by her own indulgence, she reluctantly riffled through Annabelle's drawers. Clothes from her teenaged years filled them; making a face, Mollie gazed at styles years out of date and several sizes too small. There was nothing remotely appropriate. Then she saw a T-shirt and a pair of track bottoms, along with a leather belt, laid out on the bed.

Jacob's clothes.

On top of them was a note: *In case the others aren't suitable.*

She stared at his strong, slanted handwriting, a strange tingle starting right down in her toes and spreading its warmth upwards. She hadn't expected him to be so thoughtful.

Yet why shouldn't she? Mollie asked herself. He'd been

thoughtful to the tune of half a million pounds already. Yet somehow his thoughtfulness in the little, hidden things meant even more than a scrawled cheque. She picked up the grey T-shirt, worn to softness, and held it to her face; it smelled like soap. It smelled like Jacob.

He'd been in here, just a few metres away from the bathroom, while she'd been soaking in the tub. Naked. Groaning a little, Mollie buried her face in the T-shirt. Why was she thinking this way? Feeling this way about *Jacob Wolfe*? He was so inappropriate as boyfriend material it was laughable. She couldn't even believe she'd mentally put *boyfriend* and *Jacob Wolfe* in the same sentence. She did *not* still have a stupid schoolgirl crush on him, she told herself fiercely. She didn't even want a boyfriend, or husband, or lover of any kind. Her business was going to take up all of her time and energy, and after five years of caring for her father, her emotional reserves were surely at an all-time low. She didn't need the complication of caring for another person.

But what about desire?

She couldn't ignore the fact that Jacob Wolfe was quite possibly the most attractive man she'd ever seen, or that her body responded to him in the most basic, elemental way.

Still, Mollie told herself as she slipped Jacob's T-shirt over her head, she didn't have to act on that attraction. She didn't have to do anything about desire. And she wouldn't have the opportunity anyway, because as far as she could tell Jacob didn't even like her very much.

She slipped on the track bottoms, which engulfed her, and rolling up the cuffs, she cinched them at the waist with the belt. She looked ridiculous, she knew, but it was better than wearing clothes that were two sizes too small and a decade out of date.

Taking her torch, Mollie started down the corridor, in search of the kitchen.

There was something a bit creepy about walking through

the darkened, dust-shrouded manor on her own. She wondered how Jacob felt living here. Surely a hotel or rented flat would be more comfortable. As she made her way downstairs she peeked into several rooms; some looked as if they'd been cleaned but others were frozen in time, untouched save for dust and cobwebs. She pictured Jacob in the manor, moving about these rooms, haunted by their memories, and suppressed an odd shiver.

She finally found the kitchen in the back of the house, a huge room now flickering with candlelight. Jacob had brought in several old silver candelabra and positioned them in various points around the room so the space danced with shadows.

'You made it.' Jacob turned around and in the dim light Mollie thought she saw his teeth flash white in a smile. 'I hope you didn't get lost.'

'Almost.' She smiled back. 'Actually, I just had a good long soak in the tub. It felt amazing.' She gestured to the clothes she wore. 'Thank you. This was very thoughtful.'

'I realised Annabelle's clothes were undoubtedly musty. They haven't been worn or even aired in years.'

'It's strange,' Mollie murmured, 'how forgotten everything is. I haven't been inside the house in years. I didn't realise how much had been left.'

Jacob stilled, and Mollie could feel his tension. She knew the exact moment when he released it and simply shrugged. 'Everyone made their own lives away from here.'

'I know.'

He reached for two plates, sliding her a sideways glance. 'Yes, you must know better than anyone, Mollie. You watched it all happen. You were the one who was left last of all, weren't you?' He spoke quietly, without mockery, and yet his words stung because she knew how true they were. She'd felt it, year after year, labouring alone.

'Yes,' she said quietly. 'I was.'

'Have you stayed here the whole time?' Jacob asked. He laid the plates on the breakfast bar in the centre of the kitchen. 'Did you never go anywhere, except for Italy?'

He made it sound as if she'd just been waiting, a prisoner of time and fate. Even if it had felt that way sometimes, to her own shame, she didn't like Jacob Wolfe remarking on it.

Yes, I was waiting. Waiting for my father to die.

'I went to university,' she told him stiffly. 'To study horticulture.'

'Of course. But other than that…you waited. You stayed.' He glanced at her, his eyes dark and fathomless, revealing nothing, but she felt his words like an accusation. A judgement.

'Yes,' she said in little more than a whisper. 'I stayed.' *Even if I didn't want to. Even if sometimes…* She swallowed and looked away. 'Something smells delicious,' she said, trying to keep her voice light and bright and airy. Trying desperately to change the subject.

Jacob opened the oven and removed a foil pan. 'I'm afraid I'm not much of a cook. It's just an Indian takeaway, but at least the oven runs on gas so it's warm still.'

'Thank you,' she replied, her voice still stiff. 'It's very generous of you to share your meal.' As Jacob pried off the foil lid from the chicken dish, Mollie realised she was starving. She'd been so involved in going through her father's things that she'd completely forgotten about dinner.

Jacob ladled the fragrant chicken and rice onto the two plates and then gestured to one of the high bar stools. 'Come and eat.'

Sliding on a stool opposite of him, Mollie was conscious of how intimate this felt. *Was.* All around them the kitchen flickered and glimmered with candlelight. The house yawned emptily in several acres in every direction; they were completely alone.

She took a bite of chicken. She knew that now was the

time to ask Jacob what he'd been doing all these years, why he'd left, if he'd ever spared a single thought for any of the people he'd left behind—all the questions she wanted answers to, deserved answers to, for that supposed clarity and closure. So she could move on from this place, just as all the Wolfes had, just as Jacob would again.

Yet the words stuck in her throat, in her heart. Did she really have a right to ask—and know—such things? She wasn't even part of the Wolfe family. She might have spent her whole life on the Wolfe estate, in the family's shadow, but she'd never been one of them. She knew that, had always known that. She'd been an observer, a silent witness, a peeping Tom. Never part of the family, not even remotely close. Her friendship with Annabelle and her father's faithful service were the only links to the family whose actions had played such havoc with her own life. Why should she have ever expected the Wolfes to feel any sense of obligation or responsibility to her or her father? Annabelle's offer to let them stay at the cottage had been a kindness, an act of charity that no one else had known about.

And yet Jacob obviously felt responsible; he'd shown her with that cheque. Yet she didn't want money, even if it was deserved. So just what *did* she want from Jacob Wolfe?

'So what have you been doing all this time?' she asked. Her voice sounded too loud, too bright. Jacob stilled. He was good at that, Mollie thought. She knew she'd caught him off guard only when he became more cautious, more careful, his movements both precise and predatory.

'Many things.'

'Such as?'

'Work.'

'What kind of work?'

'This and that.'

Mollie laid down her fork, exasperated by his oblique answers. 'Why don't you want to say? Was it something illegal?'

Jacob's brows snapped together in a dark frown. 'No, of course not.'

She shrugged. 'Well, how am I supposed to know? You never sent a letter or left a message. Annabelle waited—'

'I don't,' Jacob told her, his tone turning icy, 'want to talk about my sister.'

Mollie refused to back down. 'She's my friend too.'

'So I gather from the photographs plastered on her wall.' Now he sounded mocking, and Mollie flushed. She hated the thought of Jacob seeing those photos, gazing at her in so many awkward and emotional stages.

'Well, if it's not something illegal, I don't know why you can't tell me,' she resumed after a second's pause. Jacob's eyes flashed blackly.

'And I don't know why you're so curious, Miss Parker,' he drawled, his tone soft. Yet there was nothing soft about his body or expression; everything was hard. Hard and unrelenting and cold.

Mollie swallowed. Suddenly this had stopped being a conversation. It had become a battle, and one she wasn't sure she wanted to fight. She had a feeling Jacob would win. She lifted her shoulder in a shrug and lightened her tone. 'Of course I'm curious. You mentioned yourself how I'm the one who has been here for so many years. How I *waited*. And I did. I waited and I watched everyone leave, one by one, starting with you. So yes, I'd like to know what started the exodus.' Somehow, as she'd started speaking, her tone had hardened and darkened. Mollie stopped, her lips still parted in surprise at just how bitter she sounded. She felt a little flicker of shame.

'So,' Jacob said after a moment, his voice still sounding

soft and yet so very hard, 'you don't just want to know what I've been doing, but why I went.'

Mollie's breath escaped in a soft, surprised rush. She might as well see this through. 'Yes.'

Jacob leaned back, his position relaxed even though his eyes were wary and alert. 'Why don't you tell me why you think I left?' Mollie stared at him, speechless. She hadn't expected *that*. She had no idea what to say. 'Or,' Jacob suggested softly, 'I could guess what you think. I could guess what you think quite easily.'

Her mouth was dry, the food like dust. She swallowed and licked her lips. 'Could you?'

'Oh, yes,' Jacob assured her, his voice laced with laughter. Mocking, cold and cruel. 'I could. You think I left because I was bored. I'd had enough of playing daddy to my brothers and sister and I decided they could fend for themselves while I went in pursuit of my own pleasure. I never wrote a letter or called or came back at all because I just didn't care. Not about them, and certainly not about you, the ragamuffin gardener's daughter who always followed me around with her heart in her eyes.'

Mollie let out an involuntary choked cry. Even though she should have known, should have expected it, she hadn't. She hadn't thought he would be so cruel. To *her*.

'Isn't that what you thought, Mollie?' Jacob asked in a silky whisper, and in a sickening flash Mollie knew she was as cruel as he was. She'd thought everything he'd said, more than once. She'd thought it in the anger and hurt of being left behind, unimportant and forgotten. She'd judged him again and again in her own heart, condemned him without a trial, without an explanation.

And now, seeing the pain flash in Jacob's dark eyes, she suddenly wondered if she'd been wrong.

Jacob laughed. It wasn't a sound Mollie liked to hear. 'Don't bother answering,' he said as he slid off his stool and took his plate—he'd eaten everything—to the sink. 'I know what you think. Every emotion and thought is reflected in those lovely eyes.'

Those lovely eyes? Now Mollie was thrown in a completely different direction, her body suddenly tingling in response to that throwaway compliment. Jacob turned to face her, bracing one hip against the kitchen counter. The candlelight threw his face into half-shadow, flickering across his features.

'I'm sorry,' Mollie said after a moment. She didn't even know what she was apologising for, yet she felt, deep inside, that the words needed to be said. She'd made so many judgements, in her loneliness and hurt, and she shouldn't have. She didn't deserve an explanation or even an apology. Yet she still didn't know what Jacob thought...or why he'd left. And now she wanted to know, for an entirely different reason. One she couldn't quite name.

'Don't,' Jacob said brusquely. He averted his face. 'Don't apologise for the truth.'

'The truth?' Mollie repeated in confusion. 'What are you saying, Jacob?'

'I did abandon my brothers and sister,' Jacob said flatly. His voice was without emotion. 'It was a price I was willing to pay, but the cost was high.' Questions clambered in Mollie's mind. The price for what? And the cost was high— for who? His siblings? *Himself?* 'Come on,' Jacob said after a moment. He sounded resigned and yet also strangely gentle. Mollie looked up. He'd pushed away from the counter and held out his hand. Without even thinking about what she was doing, Mollie slid off the stool and took his hand.

His fingers curled around hers, warm, dry, strong. A shiver of awareness rippled from his touch all the way through her body, making her breath hitch and her blood pump and everything inside her come alive. Bubbles again, so sweet and tempting and dangerous.

'What—?'

'I want to show you something,' Jacob said. And still holding her hand, he led her from the room.

CHAPTER FOUR

JACOB hadn't meant to hold her hand. He hadn't even meant to show her what he'd found; she probably already knew, and even if she didn't, he could have slipped it in an envelope and left it on her doorstep.

He didn't want to draw closer to this woman who asked him pointed questions, and yet stared at him with a shock and hurt *he'd* caused.

Yet here he was, leading her through the shadowy corridors, his hand laced with hers, her fingers small and slender under his, trusting and fragile despite his harsh words of just a few moments ago. It felt good. Too good. It had been so long since he'd felt another human being's gentle touch. Years since he'd allowed himself to get that close to anyone. Mollie Parker drew him in with her sweetness, her softness, and even her determination and strength. He didn't want to be drawn, and yet still he was. Still he wanted.

Yet he knew he couldn't want this. Jacob had returned home for one purpose, and one purpose only: to sell the manor. Reuniting his family was a necessary and important part of that, but seducing Mollie Parker was not.

For that was all it would be. A seduction: pleasurable, pointless. That was all he ever allowed himself to have, because he knew it was all he could ever give.

He was empty inside, empty and aching. Or worse, Jacob corrected himself, he was *full*. Full of poisoned memories, treacherous regrets. Full of the truth of himself, of what he was capable of. He had nothing to give Mollie Parker. Nothing she would want.

Except a rose.

'Why are we going back here?' Mollie asked, for Jacob had led her into the study. The room still felt suffocating to her, despite the windows open to the night. The smell of rain and roses carried on the breeze.

'I found something when I was going through my father's papers,' Jacob said. He'd dropped her hand and retreated behind the big oak desk, leaving Mollie with the sweet memory of his touch. Her fingers tingled. He began to riffle through the papers on his desk. 'He had the most atrocious filing system,' he continued. 'Which of course isn't very surprising.'

'I didn't know much about your father,' Mollie said cautiously. 'Except…'

Jacob glanced up, his eyes flashing. He had stilled, again. Watchful and wary. 'Except what?' he asked quietly.

'What people said. Whispered about in the village.'

'And what did they whisper about in the village?' Jacob asked, his tone deceptively mild.

'That he was charming,' Mollie answered hesitantly, 'and a drunk.'

'He was both. Unfortunately he wasn't much of a father.'

He spoke so dispassionately, as if it hardly mattered, that Mollie was compelled to ask, 'You must regret that.'

His eyes narrowed as he looked up at her. 'I do. I've regretted it my whole life.' She heard something in his voice, a raw, jagged note she hadn't expected; it cut beneath his cold, composed exterior, hinted at the hurting man underneath. 'I regret it for my brothers and sister,' Jacob continued. 'I wasn't much of a replacement.'

'But you tried.'

He lifted one shoulder in a dismissive shrug before turning back to the papers on the desk, his manner brisk. 'My father did, amazingly, have a few redeeming qualities. Such as this.' He held out a piece of thick parchment paper, yellowed and crackling with age, towards her.

Hesitantly Mollie took it. 'What…' she began, her breath coming out in a soft rush as she gazed down at the paper. A dried rose, its petals brown and faded yet still perfect, had been affixed to the parchment. Underneath, in an unfamiliar hand, was written *The Mollie Rose*.

Her throat thickened, unexpectedly, with tears, and her fingers clenched on the fragile parchment.

'Careful,' Jacob said, and he gently loosened her fingers' death grip with his own.

'Sorry. I—I didn't— How did he—your father—get this?'

'As far as I can tell, your father showed him.' Jacob pointed to some more handwriting, smaller and slanted, underneath the rose's name.

A new hybrid Parker named after his daughter. Sweet.

'It must have touched my father in one of his more lucid moments.'

'My father was always experimenting with roses,' Mollie said in a voice she didn't quite recognise as her own. 'Sometimes I thought—it seemed—as if he cared more for them…' She shook her head, not wanting to taint her father's memory with regretful recollections. Yes, he'd loved his beloved roses, been obsessed by them even, but she'd always known he'd loved her more. She'd never doubted that, even in the darkest moments of his disease. She looked up at Jacob. 'He never told me—I never knew he named one after me.'

Jacob glanced down at the pressed petals, now leached of colour. 'I wonder what colour it was. Red, perhaps, like your hair.' He reached out to gently tuck a stray curl behind her ear. His fingers barely brushed her skin, yet Mollie felt as if they lingered. Her whole body reacted to that touch, the whisper of skin against skin. Instinctively she leaned into it. Abruptly Jacob dropped his hand, took a step back.

Mollie realised she was holding her breath, and she drew it in with an audible gulp. 'Thank you for showing me this,' she said. She tried to ignore the fact that her heart was hammering and her ear and cheek still tingled from his touch.

'You can keep it.'

'Thank you. It means a lot.'

'You were close to your father?' He sounded almost wistful.

'Yes…' Mollie realised she sounded hesitant, unsure. How could she explain the kind of relationship she had with her father? He'd adored her; she'd always known that. It had just been the two of them, together, forever, and for so long she couldn't imagine life without him.

Yet living alone with a forgetful father who was obsessed with the quality of soil and the new fertilising techniques had been difficult at times; Henry Parker had not always known when she needed new clothes, or a listening ear, or a simple hug. And then five years of dwindling into dementia had left Mollie feeling more alone and bereft than ever.

His death, in some ways, had been a relief. It was a thought that made her cringe inwardly with guilt and shame even now.

'I know it was nothing like—like your father,' she said stiltedly, 'nothing at all. But…sometimes…it was lonely.' She felt ashamed to say it, especially considering what Jacob and the other Wolfes must have endured under William's unforgiving hand.

Jacob gave her the faintest of smiles. 'We all carry our own sorrows. Just because they're different, doesn't make them any less.' He gestured to the rose. 'I'm glad you have that.'

Her throat too tight to speak, Mollie could only nod. She

felt humbled by Jacob's willingness to accept her own pain. He could have easily shrugged it off, told her she had no idea, nothing to cry about....

Or was that just how *she* felt?

She looked up and saw that Jacob was regarding her with a certain thoughtfulness that made her think he saw too much. Knew too much.

And she didn't know anything.

'Tell me about him,' she said, and he stiffened.

'There's not much worth telling,' he said after a moment. Mollie was glad he didn't pretend to misunderstand. She was talking about William Wolfe, his father, the author of his own sorrows. The man he'd accidentally killed—and must have hated. 'I wish...' Jacob said, and then stopped.

'Wished...?' Mollie prompted softly.

'I wish there was more to tell,' Jacob said, a brusque note entering his voice. 'I wish I had—we all had—more happy memories with him. I wish my siblings had had a proper father, rather than—' He stopped abruptly, but Mollie, just as before, felt she could have finished his thought. *Rather than me*. He gave her a bleak smile. 'If wishes were horses, eh?'

'Something like that.' The intimacy of the moment still seemed to wrap around them. 'Annabelle never spoke about him,' Mollie said quietly. 'Not that I asked. I was only eight when—'

'He died.' Jacob's voice was flat, cold. Mollie realised she shouldn't have said anything. They could have moved on, away from this startling intimacy, the sharing of memories, secrets. Yet even now she didn't want to. She wanted to know.

'It must have been so hard,' she whispered. 'For you, especially.' Jacob flinched at her words. Mollie wished she knew what to say. No words seemed adequate, appropriate, so she said the only thing she could think of, the only thing she knew she really meant. 'I'm sorry,' she whispered.

'I told you, you don't need to apologise for the truth,' Jacob told her. His expression hardened into something unfriendly and even mean. It was hard to believe that a moment ago he'd made her heart beat with awareness and desire. Now, taking in his tightened mouth and narrowed eyes, so endlessly dark, it hammered with something close to fear—yet not for herself. She was afraid for *him*. 'The truth,' he continued in the same brutal tone, 'was that he was an utter bastard. He terrorised his wives and his children, he drank away the family's money, and when he died I felt—' He stopped suddenly, his face twisted in an agony of grief. He drew a shuddering breath and looked away, every muscle tensed.

'Jacob...' Mollie said, inadvertently, instinctively, for something deep in her called to the brokenness she saw in the man before her. She lifted her arms, reaching out as if to do—what? *Hug* him? Even though she knew Jacob Wolfe would probably be appalled by the thought of a hug, she couldn't help herself. She wanted to reach him. Touch him.

His face cleared, as if a veil had been drawn across that deeper, darker emotion; he hid the broken edges, the jagged memories, and coated them with blandness. 'You asked,' he said. 'And now you know.' His mouth curved in a slow smile. 'Satisfied, Mollie?' he asked, touching her cheek with one finger. Mollie jerked under the caress, for that was surely what it was. Slowly, thoughtfully, his face still a hard mask, Jacob trailed his finger down her cheek, igniting sparks of awareness along her jaw, to the sensitive curve of her neck. He lingered there, his finger touching her pulse, a witness to its frantic hammering.

Mollie remained rooted to the spot, amazed at how such a simple, little touch could affect her so utterly. So disastrously. She felt as she was filled with bubbles once again, bubbles made of the most fragile glass, and they were popping one by one. She didn't know what would be left when they were gone. She didn't know what would happen, what could happen.

What Jacob wanted to happen.

He watched her carefully, noting her reaction, and in her appalled shame Mollie wondered how the mood could have changed so suddenly, how the charged atmosphere of anger and regret had turned so quickly to something just as dangerous.

She swallowed convulsively as Jacob rested just one finger in the curve of her neck, stroking that smooth, secretive skin lightly, as if he were learning a landmark. And she didn't move away. Didn't protest. Didn't do anything except submit, her body yearning for his deeper caress.

After a long, pulsating moment, the only sound the hitch of her own breath, he trailed his finger from that curve to her collarbone, pausing to stroke the hard ridge of bone, the skin stretched so achingly taut over it, and then let it drop lightly yet quite deliberately to the V of her T-shirt—*his* T-shirt.

Mollie heard her sharply in-drawn breath as his finger nestled there in the soft dip between her breasts, stroking the skin softly, as if asking a question.

She felt heat flood through her—and he was touching her with only one finger! She glanced up and saw the clinical, detached look on his face and shame replaced that liquefying heat. He wasn't affected at all.

'Don't—' she whispered. She didn't even know what she wanted to stop, the look on Jacob's face or the touch of his hand. Her body certainly didn't want him to stop; her body wanted hands, mouths, lips. Everywhere, everything.

'Don't what?' Jacob asked in a voice of lethal softness.

'Don't tease me,' Mollie said, for surely that was what he was doing. He used seduction—sex—like a weapon, the most powerful one he had. She wished she had the strength to step away but she didn't. She closed her eyes, briefly, in silent supplication, then opened them. She drew a steady breath. 'What do you want from me, Jacob?'

'Now, that's an interesting question.' Smiling faintly, Jacob drew his finger back along her collarbone, up her neck and then lightly across one cheek. She felt as if he'd marked her, as if she'd see a livid red line where he'd touched. She even glanced down at herself to check; there was nothing.

His hand rested on her cheek, his thumb caressing the fullness of her lips. 'I'm attracted to you, Mollie,' he said, and inside she quavered at the knowledge, both with wonder and trepidation. 'And you're attracted to me.' His thumb rested fully on her mouth; she couldn't speak even if she wanted to. 'We're alone here, for the foreseeable future. Why not make the most of it?'

He sounded so reasonable, so affable, so bland. *Why not make the most of it?* As if it could—or would—be so simple and easy. She knew it would not. She knew Jacob knew it too; she could see it in the blazing blackness of his eyes. He was provoking her with this seductive suggestion. It was a challenge, a reaction to her intrusive questions, her instinctive sympathy. It wasn't the easy suggestion he made it sound. It was a punishment.

Somehow she found the strength to step away; Jacob let his hand fall, easily, without regret or apology. 'You mean an affair,' she stated flatly.

He paused, his eyes narrowing slightly. 'Call it what you will.'

'No strings,' she clarified, because even though it was so obvious she still had to say it. Jacob Wolfe was not a man who cultivated relationships.

'None.'

And for one gloriously tempting moment, despite the dark reasons for his suggestion that she could only guess, she could imagine it. Every nerve and sinew of her body clamoured for it, because when had she ever indulged in something so sensual, so basic and pleasurable, as an affair? She'd had a few mediocre relationships in university, but nothing that remotely came close to what Jacob Wolfe was offering. And for the past five years she'd been living the life of a reclusive nun, caring for her father, working as much as she could, barely able to make ends meet. Even in Italy she'd been too busy visiting gardens and healing her own grief to really pay attention to any men.

Yet here was Jacob Wolfe, darkly dangerous, utterly beautiful, suggesting they have an affair.

Sex.

It was outrageous. Incredible. A little alarming.

Tempting.

And yet she couldn't do it. And she knew Jacob knew it too. Perhaps that was the only reason he'd suggested it in the first place.

She'd seen something in Jacob's eyes, something real and dark and wounded, and knew that she couldn't get involved with this man. Couldn't keep her body and heart separate. Jacob Wolfe would hurt her. Maybe he wouldn't mean to, maybe he wouldn't want to, but he would.

She would let him. She didn't know how to have a no-strings affair, and she wasn't about to start with a man like Jacob Wolfe.

'I...I can't.' She took another step away, and then another. Jacob didn't say anything; in the shadowy room she couldn't quite make out his expression. And she suddenly didn't want to know it, didn't want to wait for his mocking reply. So she did the only thing she could think of, the only avenue left to her.

She ran.

Jacob watched Mollie flee the room, heard the distant slam of a door. He pictured her stumbling through the gardens, tripping on tree roots, her hair a molten stream behind her.

What a mess. What a mess he'd made. And he'd done it intentionally, out of a sense of self-preservation so basic and elemental. It had been a warning, both to her and himself: *don't get close to me. I don't know what I'll do. What I'm capable of.*

Sighing heavily, he pushed away from the desk and nearly stepped on the parchment Mollie had dropped in her surprise and distress.

The Mollie Rose.

Jacob had no idea what had possessed his father to preserve the rose like some child's drawing; all he could think was that his father had been in one of his rare, sweetly lucid moments. Like when he'd built them a tree house, or brought them Christmas hampers from Hartington's. Moments the children had revelled in with hesitant incredulity, they'd been so rare. Of course, when he'd burned the tree house down a week later, or destroyed the hamper's contents in a drunken rage, Jacob was the one left picking up the pieces, taking the hits.

Until that one night, when he'd refused. In that moment of defence—*defiance*—he'd ended one life and changed everyone else's for ever.

He sighed again, the sound halfway to a groan, hating that these memories still claimed him. Over the years he'd pushed them so far down he could almost pretend they didn't exist. Had never happened.

Almost.

In dreams they taunted him. They claimed him and made him their captive.

And now, back at Wolfe Manor, it was worse than ever. He felt them rise up inside of him, felt the ghosts clamour around him, whisper their taunts in his ears.

You're a thug. A drunk. A murderer. There's no good in you at all. You hurt everyone who comes close.

And he'd proved that yet again, when he just tried to

seduce one of the sweetest, most innocent women he'd ever met. He recalled the look of astonishment and even hurt in Mollie's eyes when he'd suggested their no-strings affair, the exact thing he'd intended not to do, knowing Mollie would refuse. Knowing she'd be bewildered, offended. Knowing it was *wrong*.

And yet he'd done it. And Jacob knew why.

She'd asked too many questions. Drawn too close. Seen something inside of him he wouldn't even acknowledge to himself.

Jacob—

She'd reached for him, and he'd almost wanted to go, to find comfort and safety in her arms. What a joke.

So he'd done the one thing he knew would make her back off. Run away, even.

He'd propositioned her.

Jacob straightened, shaking off the thoughts and recriminations. He closed his mind, allowed a comforting, controlled blankness to steal over him in a numbing fog. He felt his heart rate slow, his body still. He took a deep breath and let it out slowly. *Better.*

Striding from the room with grimly focused purpose, he told himself what had happened was a good thing. At least he wouldn't be seeing Mollie Parker for a while.

Mollie ran all the way home, her chest heaving, her sides aching. She didn't stop until she was in the cottage, the door slammed and bolted, as if Jacob was the big bad wolf and she was Little Red Riding Hood.

She laughed humourlessly at her rather bad pun. Jacob *was* a Wolfe, and he *had* been chasing her, after a fashion. Unlike Little Red Riding Hood, however, she hadn't stood her ground.

The electricity had thankfully come back on, and Mollie quickly put the kettle on and built up the fire. She stripped off Jacob's clothes and kicked them in a corner, knowing she would have to wash and return them at some point but not able to think of it now.

A cup of tea would soothe her. Stabilise her. A cup of tea, Mollie thought as she swathed herself in her father's old terry robe, could make everything better.

Yet when she had finally seated herself in the rickety rocking chair by the fire, a steaming mug cradled in her hands, she felt neither stabilised nor soothed.

She felt like a complete ninny.

What would Jacob think of her, running from the room like a spooked little girl, a frightened child? Why on earth couldn't she have said something cutting and clever, worldly and wise? Instead she'd blushed and stammered and *ran*.

Groaning, Mollie leaned her head against the back of her chair as the memory of what had just happened washed over her in a shaming wave. She hadn't had enough experience of men, of *people*, in the past five years to be able to handle a proposition like Jacob's with the ease and grace she wanted to. For too long the only person she'd really talked to had been her father, and he hadn't always been able to remember her name. The heavy toll of the past five years weighed on her now, crippled her with its memory. She wanted to throw it off, had been about to throw it off when she'd returned from Italy, yet with Jacob's return and her enforced stay at Wolfe Manor she found herself spinning on the same endless wheel as before. Only this time she spun alone.

Tears—sudden, stupid—pricked her eyes. When was she going to get over the hand life had dealt her? When would she come to terms with the pain and loss of her parents' deaths and her own resulting loneliness? When could she start to live out the dreams she'd woven so optimistically, dreams she'd detailed and embroidered during her time in Italy, when she'd been so ready to take up the reins of her life again and really start living?

Now they felt completely wrecked, their fragile threads unravelling and frayed.

Restlessly Mollie rose from the rocking chair, her mug forgotten on the side table. The cottage felt cramped, its walls pressing in on her with its memories and regrets. She could almost picture her father standing by the door, dressed in his work clothes, expecting to walk out into the gardens he'd loved like another child, Wolfe Manor in its heyday. Instead she'd had to lull him back to this very rocking chair, take off his boots and tell him lies about how it was raining or a holiday because he didn't understand the truth: Wolfe Manor was falling apart and the only people left amidst the shambles were the two of them.

Master William needs me, Mollie. He's expecting me.

Sometimes her father had remembered that William was dead, that the children were fatherless: *Master Jacob needs help, Mollie. We need to help him the best way we can, by tending the gardens in our care....*

Yet by then Jacob had been long gone, as had all the other Wolfe children. Save Annabelle, none of them had said goodbye. None of them had even really known she or her father existed.

Groaning aloud, Mollie shook her head as if she could banish the painful memories. She'd spent too much time in this cottage, watching, wondering, waiting. Too much time in these gardens, caring for someone else's land. She had to get out of here. Now.

She didn't even bother with a coat, just slipped on her boots and headed out into the damp night. A chilly wind blew over her, cooling her heated face. She veered away from the landscaped gardens and headed instead for the lake. She hadn't been to the lake since she'd returned to Wolfe Manor; it was far from the house and not necessarily in the realm of the gardens. Family lore said it was haunted, that someone had once drowned in it. Even the villagers regarded it with a certain amount of suspicion. Now its smooth black surface gleamed darkly under the moon, and a few weedy reeds grew at its edge. Mollie stood there for a while, breathing in the cool, fresh night air, letting it fill her lungs and buoy her sagging spirit.

She couldn't change anything about the past, not the way her mother had died when she was born, or her father's lingering illness, or even the way she'd responded to Jacob that very night.

But she could change the future. The future—her own fate—was in her hands, and only hers, and she intended to make some changes. Starting tomorrow she would reclaim her dreams. She'd get her own life back, the life she'd envisaged in Italy, the life she had been dreaming for years of having. Independent, purposeful, far from Wolfe Manor. She took another breath and let it out slowly, and then she turned from the still waters of the lake and headed back to the cottage.

She nearly tripped over the envelope that had been left on the flagstone doorstep. Picking it up, Mollie slid out a piece of parchment. Her rose. And she realised that Jacob must have delivered it while she'd been out at the lake.

They'd both been unable to sleep, wandering in the dark, lost in memories. At that moment she felt a sorrowful companionship with him, one she'd never expected to feel. Slipping the parchment back into its envelope, she headed inside, knowing that no matter how close she and Jacob might be in some matters, he was still a stranger to her.

The next morning was one of those fresh, clean days that only came after a rainstorm. The sunlight glinted off every puddle, made the trees and leaves shimmer with dew. Dressed in her smartest pair of trousers and a pretty, feminine top of pale lavender, Mollie headed over to the manor. She wore clothes she'd bought in Italy, and they felt like armour. Weapons to reclaim the life she'd envisaged for herself, before Jacob Wolfe had scattered all her plans.

She lifted the heavy brass knocker on the manor's front door and let it fall, the sound echoing sonorously through the empty house. After a long, tense moment, Jacob opened the door.

Mollie's gaze swept over him in an instant; he was dressed in a pair of loose grey trousers and a black T-shirt that clung to the defined muscles of his chest and torso, and his hair was damp with sweat. He didn't smile.

'I'm sorry,' she said. 'Were you busy?'

'Nothing too important.' Jacob didn't move to let her pass. His tone, Mollie decided, verged on unfriendly. 'May I help you with something?'

'I need to talk to you.'

He hesitated, and she realised he didn't want to let her inside. Had she offended him by running away? Or just bored him? 'If it's about last night,' he finally said, 'I apologise. I never should have suggested such a thing.'

And even though Mollie knew she should only feel relief, she felt disappointment. Ridiculous, but real. 'It's not about that,' she said, her voice stiff with awkwardness. 'Although thank you for your apology.'

Jacob lifted one shoulder in a shrug. He still didn't move. Mollie felt the beginnings of a tension headache, as well as a growing sense of exasperation. 'Could you please let me in? I prefer not to have conversations on doorsteps.'

Jacob waited another long moment, so Mollie thought he might actually refuse. Out of instinct she placed one hand flat on the door, as if she was afraid he'd shut it in her face. At this gesture, Jacob gave her the faintest flicker of a smile and stepped aside.

'Come into the kitchen,' he said as he led her down a long narrow corridor. 'It's the most habitable room in the house.'

This morning the kitchen was awash in sunlight, not flickering with tempting shadows as it had been the night before. Mollie saw the two plates from their dinner were washed and stacked by the sink, and the aroma of coffee scented the air.

'Would you like some?' Jacob asked, gesturing to the pot on the worktop.

She nodded. Best to keep this professional. A business meeting, over coffee. 'Yes, please.'

Jacob poured her a mug and handed her the cream and sugar bowl before pouring his own, which he sipped black. He arched one eyebrow. 'How may I help you, Mollie?'

She got shivers every time he called her by name. It wasn't often. Yet there was something strangely, sweetly intimate about hearing Jacob saying her name, as if it were a choice he made rather than a simple form of address.

She pushed the thought away; it would hardly help her now. 'I want to resign this commission.' Jacob's expression didn't flicker and Mollie went doggedly on. 'It's too big a job for me. You need someone more experienced.'

'I disagree.'

'You don't even know,' Mollie returned, frustration firing her words. 'Do you have any experience with garden design?' She'd meant to scoff, but Jacob took the question seriously.

He cocked his head. 'A bit.'

Mollie blew out her breath in exasperation. 'Well, even so, I can't do it.'

'You made an agreement.'

'I didn't sign anything.'

His eyebrow arched higher. 'I thought your word was enough.'

Mollie flushed. He'd backed her into a corner and she hated it. She needed more *space*. 'You could find someone else very easily,' she said. She heard the desperation creeping into her voice. 'Someone more qualified—'

'I told you, I never should have suggested there be anything between us but a professional business arrangement,' Jacob said. His voice was cool, with a bite of impatience. 'So if you're worried—'

'No.' Her face felt on fire, right to the roots of her hair. She must look like a carrot. 'It's not that.' Jacob didn't answer, and Mollie knew he wasn't convinced. He must think her the gauchest kind of girl, she thought miserably. She'd run away last night, and she'd marched here in the morning to resign. Yet Jacob's offer—tempting, treacherous—had been a catalyst, not the reason. She swallowed. Now was the time for honesty. 'It really isn't, Jacob.' His name sounded strange on her lips. Another intimacy. 'It's this house. All the memories. Don't you feel them?' She had instinctively dropped her voice to a whisper, as if the ghosts crowded around them, listening. Jacob stared at her, utterly still. His eyes had widened, his mouth parted slightly.

'Yes,' he said after a long moment, his voice quiet and sad. 'I do. But I didn't think you did.'

Mollie could only imagine what kind of memories tormented Jacob. Actually, she *couldn't* imagine. Her upbringing had had its own sorrows, as Jacob had acknowledged, but nothing like what he must have experienced. Her one experience of William Wolfe told her that. How could she fault him for wanting to leave such an unhappy place? She wanted to now. She'd wanted to years ago.

'Mine are different than yours,' she said slowly. 'My father loved me, and I loved him, but—' She drew a breath, made herself continue. 'For the past five years I'd been nursing him through dementia. I didn't want to put him in a care facility, because I knew he'd be happiest here, where he spent all of his life. But…it was hard.' She tried to smile, but felt her mouth wobble instead. She didn't like to talk about her lonely years with her father, and who wanted to hear about it anyway? She saw Annabelle so rarely these days that even her closest friend barely knew what Mollie had been enduring. 'Really hard,' she continued after a pause, 'and really lonely. I went to Italy because I needed a change.'

'I'm sorry,' Jacob said quietly. 'I can only imagine how difficult it must have been to stay.' His words held a certain poignancy, as well as a silent acknowledgement of the fact that he *hadn't* stayed. He really could only imagine.

'Anyway,' she said, trying to inject a firm, bright note into her voice, 'I never intended to stay in the cottage for more than a few days. I wanted to pack up my things—and my dad's things—and let a place in the village, as I told you that first night.' Jacob made no reply, and Mollie continued, her voice finally sounding firm, 'And that's what I need to do. Being here—alone—is too difficult for me. I came back from Italy planning a fresh start, and that's what I'm going to do.'

Jacob said nothing for a long moment. Mollie didn't either; she'd said all she could.

'How can you start fresh,' Jacob asked after a moment, 'without first dealing with the past?' Mollie had the odd feeling he was talking as much to himself as he was to her.

'Is that why you came back?' she asked.

'Partly.' He took a sip of coffee. 'The other reason was the house was violating building codes.' He smiled wryly, lightening the moment just a little, and Mollie smiled back, although part of her longed to ask Jacob more. She knew he wouldn't give her answers. 'Don't go, Mollie,' Jacob said quietly. 'Don't run away. You stayed all those years, when it was far harder than it is now. Finish the job not for me, or for your career, or the manor, but for yourself and your father. Restore these gardens to the glory he once knew, and walk away proud. You'll be glad you did.'

Tears pricked her eyes. She hadn't expected *that*. She'd been prepared to argue with a coolly mocking Jacob, not with this man whose heart, for once, seemed reflected in his eyes. They weren't endlessly black; they held their own light coming from deep within. 'And what about you?' she whispered. 'Will you walk away proud?'

Jacob didn't answer for a long time. Mollie saw the shadows cloud his eyes once more, the darkness that hid a pain she couldn't yet understand. 'I'll walk away,' he finally said, and his voice was flat enough to make Mollie not question his words.

CHAPTER FIVE

SHE stayed. Mollie wondered if she'd ever really intended to leave. Certainly the desperate impulse had been abandoned from the moment she'd heard Jacob's heartfelt words. All it had taken was one quiet plea and she'd melted.

And, she was honest enough to acknowledge, there was truth in what he'd said. It was why she'd accepted the commission in the first place; she wanted to see the gardens restored. She wanted to do it herself. Then she'd be able to move on with a clear conscience and a light heart.

If she survived.

Yet she hardly needed to worry about Jacob tempting her yet again, for he kept his distance as June bled into July. Mollie occupied herself with work. There was so much of it, and even though she hired some men from the village to do the heaviest jobs, she could still stay in the gardens from dawn to dusk and never have an idle moment.

She'd yet to consider how to redesign the parts of the estate that could not be restored, like the Rose Garden. She walked along the octagonal pathways and inspected the rose bushes, now dry and shrivelled, wondering how she could replace something that had been one of the estate's crowning glories, her father's proudest achievement. She'd sketched some ideas, perused catalogues of the latest hybrids and perennials, yet anything she came up with seemed a poor second to what had already been there. How could there not be a Rose Garden at all?

Still, the work of simply restoring the gardens to what they had once been was enough to occupy her, both mind and body.

Almost. Her mind—and her body—still wandered away from the task at hand, wondered what Jacob was doing. Thinking. Feeling. Wondered how it would feel if he kissed her, if she told him she'd changed her mind and she wanted his no-strings affair after all.

Mollie knew she never would. Not only was such a possibility still too dangerous, it was also terrifying to imagine Jacob's cool rejection. What if he'd changed his mind? What if he didn't want her after all? What if that suggestion had been nothing more than a mockery?

And since he stayed away from her week after week, that seemed more than a possibility; it was surely a likelihood.

And a good thing too, Mollie told herself. She didn't need complications. She didn't need Jacob Wolfe.

Even if she wanted him.

In early July, when the country was in the grip of an unexpected heatwave so the very air seemed to shimmer, he found her in the Rose Garden. She'd gone there, as she often did, to pace those familiar pathways and wonder just what she was going to do. She'd reluctantly removed the rose bushes and turned over the earth; the beds were ready for planting. She just didn't know what to plant.

'You look like you're trying to solve a particular complicated maths problem.'

Mollie whirled around, her heart already starting to thump at the sound of Jacob's voice. He stood in the entrance to the little garden, the hedges dark around him. He wore jeans and a faded T-shirt, yet even in such casual clothes he looked amazing. Mollie drank him in, her gaze lingering on the sinewy muscles of his arms and chest, the way the jeans emphasised his trim hips and powerful thighs, the loose grace of every movement.

She realised she was staring and jerked her gaze away. 'Something like that. I'm trying to decide what to plant in this garden.'

Jacob glanced at the empty beds. 'This was the Rose Garden, wasn't it?'

'Yes,' she said. 'There have been roses here for five hundred years.'

'Time for a change, then.'

She laughed; she'd honestly never thought of it that way. 'I suppose,' she said. 'We can't plant roses, at any rate.'

'Why not?'

'The soil is depleted. That's what made the plants vulnerable in the first place. After a long time, even new rose bushes will fail to thrive if they're planted in soil where roses have been before.'

'Rather difficult creatures, aren't they?'

A smile tugged at Mollie's mouth, surprising her. 'Yes,' she agreed, 'they are. Temperamental and fragile and damned hard to grow.'

'So it seems like something else should grow here.'

'Every manor house has a rose garden,' Mollie said. Jacob arched an eyebrow.

'All the more reason not to have one, I'd say.'

'You are a contrary person, aren't you?' Mollie said, half teasing, half serious. He shrugged, offering her that faint, cool smile.

'So some people say.'

A silence descended, awkward and uncertain, and Mollie gazed at the empty flower beds, trying to think of something—anything—to say. 'What have you been doing?' she finally blurted. 'I haven't seen you around.'

'I've been busy.' His tone was cool and a bit impersonal,

and Mollie knew that he was keeping her from asking more questions. Yet somehow she just couldn't help herself.

'You mentioned before that you went to London on business. And you have an assistant, so you're obviously engaged in some kind of work.' She tried to keep her voice light, friendly. 'What is it that you do, Jacob?'

He hesitated, and Mollie wondered why he was so reluctant to tell her. Then he gave a little laugh and said, 'I don't mean to be so much the man of mystery. I'm an architect actually.'

'An architect?' Mollie remembered that he had said he was overseeing the renovation himself. 'J Design,' she realised aloud, and saw Jacob's expression flicker before he spread his hands and smiled.

'You sussed me out.'

She shook her head in disbelief. 'J Design is an amazing company. You work for them?' He didn't answer, and Mollie thought of the five hundred thousand pounds he'd been able to give away with such ease. 'You started it,' she stated. 'You're the founder. *J* is for Jacob.' He gave a shrug of acknowledgement, and Mollie let out a little laugh.

'And I told you they were quite good!' She laughed again at the absurdity of it, and was gladdened to see Jacob smile back. 'But that's fantastic. Why do you hide it?'

'I've been a very private person for many years,' Jacob said after a moment. 'I suppose it's hard to stop.'

The nineteen years Jacob had spent away seemed to lie between them, heavy with memories and experiences she could neither know nor understand. And none of his family had known either. At least Annabelle hadn't.

Yet Annabelle had forgiven Jacob; that much was clear in her emails to Mollie. She simply wanted to see her family reunited and happy once more. Mollie was the one who had wanted explanations, apologies, and she deserved neither. Not as much as the Wolfes did anyway.

'I thought I should give you these,' Jacob said, finally breaking the silence. He held a bulky plastic bag aloft, and Mollie took it with surprise.

'What is it?'

'Something I thought you needed.'

Mollie peeked in the bag and saw a spectacular pair of high-end rubber boots. With purple polka dots. She thought of the way the ripped seam in her boot had leaked muddy water across Jacob's rug, and she looked up, both touched and unsettled. He noticed everything—and he did something about it. 'Thank you. That's incredibly thoughtful. And I suppose I should, in kind, give you a new entry rug.'

Jacob gave her the glimmer of a smile. 'Hardly necessary. That rug was nearing the end of its life as it was. You simply dealt the necessary death blow.' His words seemed to echo between them, and Mollie saw how he stiffened. She'd stiffened too.

Death blow. The words—the innocent expression—brought to mind a crowd of ugly, unpleasant memories.

'Well, thank you,' she finally said again. 'Really.'

'There's something else,' Jacob said.

Mollie raised her eyebrows in surprise. 'Oh?'

'I'm going to London tomorrow for a design expo. J Design is featuring some of its newest projects, along with several other architectural firms. There will also be a land-scaping element that I thought would interest you.'

Mollie blinked. 'Me?'

'Yes,' Jacob said, and she heard humour—rare, precious— in his voice. 'I'm asking you to go with me.'

Jacob had made the decision to ask Mollie to accompany him quite suddenly. He'd fully intended to keep out of her way until her work on the gardens was finished, and so far he'd managed that. Occasionally he spied her from the study window, a flash of coppery hair amidst the vivid tangle of green in the garden, and something in him constricted, an unfulfilled ache he knew was more than just simple lust.

All the more reason to stay out of her way.

Yet when the expo came up, and he saw the landscaping displays, he thought of her, thought of how the manor seemed as much a prison to her as it was to him. And for a few days they could both break out of it.

That was the only reason he was asking her, Jacob told himself. Out of kindness. Pity, even.

He'd lived too long in the confines of his own mind to believe such self-deception.

Yet he refused to think of what the other reasons could be.

Now he watched as surprise flashed in her soft brown eyes, turning them golden, and she bit the pink, rosebud fullness of her lower lip in obvious uncertainty. She hadn't expected to be asked. She probably wondered why he was asking. Was she afraid he'd proposition her again?

He wouldn't. Of that Jacob was certain. He surely had enough control over his own mind and body to keep from embarrassing and frightening her again.

Yet he couldn't keep himself from wanting to spend a little more time with her, to revel in her soft beauty even if he knew she was out of bounds. He *liked* just being with her, Jacob knew; she saw something in him that no one else saw. And while that thought half terrified him, it also made him want more. Want to be known and understood, even the darkest, most hidden parts of himself—the *truth* of himself—he was afraid ever to reveal.

Now, *that* was surely pushing things too far.

'Go with you?' Mollie repeated. She heard the blatant surprise in her voice and blushed. Her heart had already started thudding again, and her palms grew slick with nerves. Already images were dancing through her mind, a hazy montage of seductive possibilities that had no business taking up space in her brain. 'To London?' she clarified, because she had no idea what to say.

'Yes, to London.' Jacob shoved his hands in the pockets of his jeans, and Mollie couldn't help but notice how the action emphasised the broadness of his shoulders, the T-shirt clinging to the ridged muscles of his abdomen. She swallowed and looked away. Already she knew how dangerous such a trip would be. London. With *Jacob*. 'I have a suite at the Grand Wolfe,' Jacob continued, naming his brother Sebastian's flagship hotel. 'The expo goes over two days, so we'd need to stay the night.' He cleared his throat. 'I don't want you to be—'

'No,' Mollie said quickly. She really didn't want to hear Jacob assure her yet again that he had no intention or interest in making his no-strings affair offer another time. 'I'm not— Don't worry…you don't need to be—' She was babbling, and she swallowed hard. Jacob smiled, a sensual tugging of his mouth that Mollie neither expected nor was prepared for. His eyes glinted darkly, and she suspected he knew how frazzled she was. She watched his lips quirk upwards, mesmerised by the simple movement, how it transformed Jacob's face, lightened it, so the shadows fell away. She wished he smiled more. She was glad, fiercely so, that she had made him smile now, even if it was to her own embarrassment.

'All right,' he said lightly. 'I won't.'

'Sorry,' Mollie mumbled, and Jacob reached out and brushed her cheek. It took Mollie a few stunned seconds to realise he was simply brushing away a smudge of dirt. Even so her heart hammered all the more and her cheek tingled.

'I've told you,' he said softly, 'you don't need to be sorry for the truth.'

But I don't know what the truth—about you—is. Mollie swallowed the words and just nodded.

'Anyway, it could be fun,' Jacob said, smiling again. 'And inspirational. The landscaping displays are meant to be quite good. And I think we could both use some time away from this place.'

Mollie nodded again. She seemed incapable of managing a coherent sentence, yet she agreed with everything he said. She knew there were things to think about, worry about, questions and concerns and dangers. Yet in that moment all she wanted to feel was the bubbles that raced through her like champagne, that made her feel excited and alive in a way she hadn't felt in years. 'Yes,' she said, firmly, quickly. 'I'd love to go with you.'

It was surprisingly easy to leave. She left instructions with the men from the village and packed a single bag. She decided she wanted to feel smart—never mind what Jacob thought—and so she threw in her clothes from Italy, including a sexy little cocktail dress in a shimmery lavender silk that she surely wouldn't have any need for. Even so, she tucked it underneath her trousers and then closed the lid of her case, zipping it firmly.

Jacob had told her to meet him up at the manor at nine, and so, lugging her case behind her, Mollie headed through the gardens, now neat and trimmed and ready for planting, towards the house.

She stopped in surprise when she saw the red convertible, parked in the circular drive. Jacob stood next to it, the keys in his hand. He looked relaxed and comfortable in a pair of tan khakis and a white button-down shirt, open at the throat. Mollie couldn't quite take her eyes from the base of his throat, the skin looking so warm and sun-kissed that she wanted to touch it. Touch *him*. She determinedly turned towards the convertible.

'Nice car.'

'Not when it rains.' Jacob responded with a grin as he reached for her case. 'Sorry, I should have picked you up at the cottage. I'm not even sure how to get there by car, though. Is there a road?'

'No, just a path.'

Jacob put her case in the car's boot and then went round to open Mollie's door. She slipped into the sumptuous interior, feeling as if she were Alice and had fallen down the rabbit hole into an unimaginable world of luxury. Jacob slid into the driver's seat and turned on the engine, which purred smoothly to life.

As Jacob pulled away from the house, the wind ruffled Mollie's hair and the sun was warm on her face. She leaned her head back against the seat and closed her eyes.

'I never even knew about that cottage until the night I saw you,' he said. Mollie opened her eyes.

'Not many people did. It was Annabelle's idea to let us stay on after you'd left. She said no one would even notice we were there.' She knew she was speaking a bit defensively; even now Jacob's implication that she'd been freeloading off his family rankled just a little. Jacob, however, did not rise to the challenge of her words.

'How did it feel to be invisible?' he asked softly as he slid her a sideways glance that managed to be all too knowing.

Surprised by his perception, Mollie let out a little laugh and looked away. 'I'm not sure I knew anything else,' she said. She didn't want to sound self-pitying, so she cleared her throat and added more robustly, 'There are worse things to be, in any case.' She paused, then dared to add, 'I'm sure you wanted to be invisible on occasion.'

He shrugged. 'Not so much me,' he said, 'as everyone else.'

'You mean your father?'

He gave a short laugh. 'That might have been handy, but no. My brothers and sister. If they'd been invisible...' He lapsed into silence, his fingers tightening on the wheel, and Mollie felt a little aching tug on her heart. No one should have such regret in their voice, etched into the lines on their face.

'You couldn't save them all,' she said quietly. She spoke the words from instinct; what did she really know about Jacob and his family? Only what Annabelle had told her, which wasn't very much at all. Jacob had been her big brother; he'd tried to protect her from her father's blows which had ended in her scar and William Wolfe's death. He'd left just a year after William's death; his absence had created an aching void in the family. Those were the bare facts, yet Mollie knew she had no idea what had gone on in the Wolfe family, day after day. How had they endured their father's drunken fits and rages? How had Jacob endured? As the oldest and the most responsible, what had he suffered? What had he *felt*? And what had finally driven him to leave?

'I didn't save them all,' Jacob said flatly, interrupting her tumultuous thoughts. 'I didn't save anyone.'

'You can't save anyone,' Mollie told him, her voice surprisingly fierce. 'I learned that with my dad. I couldn't save him from dementia or death. I could only ease the way.' She laid a hand on his arm, the skin warm under her fingers. Warm and tense. 'You take too much on yourself, Jacob.'

She felt the muscles leap and jerk under her hand and he threw her a scoffing sideways glance. 'You speak as though you have years of experience.'

She knew he was trying to draw away from her, to hide behind mockery. She shrugged. 'A few years, at least.'

Jacob didn't speak for a moment, and his silence felt like an acknowledgement. 'You don't know anything about me, Mollie,' he finally said, his voice quiet and a little sad. 'Or what I am. Our experiences are entirely different.'

'Then tell me. Tell me about yourself.'

He pressed his lips together. 'I'm not sure much bears repeating.'

'Tell me how you started J Design, then,' Mollie said. She

refused to be put off. 'That's a story worth telling, I should think.'

'I fell into it, more or less,' Jacob said. He flexed his arms, his hands on the wheel, and Mollie could tell how uncomfortable the whole conversation made him. He wasn't a man used to talking—or even thinking—about himself. 'I did some building work, and had a look at the designs. I thought I could improve them, and so I tried. The developer liked my suggestions, and it sort of went from there.'

Mollie thought it sounded like an incredibly oversimplified version of what she was sure would be an engrossing and inspiring story, but she decided not to press. 'J Design does a lot of work for charity, doesn't it? Is that your choice?'

'I like to help those less fortunate,' Jacob replied with a shrug. He glanced at her, his eyes narrowing. 'I noticed you haven't cashed your cheque.'

'Am I less fortunate, then?' Mollie asked lightly, although his implication stung just a little.

'That's not what I meant. Although I consider it *un*fortunate that your father worked for so long without being paid. Why didn't you deposit the cheque?'

Mollie shrugged. 'It didn't feel right.'

'You deserve that money, Mollie—'

'Do I?' she challenged quietly. 'I might have flung a few accusations at you, but the truth is my father didn't work a full day for years. He was too ill.'

'And why do I think that you carried his slack?' Jacob questioned, his voice soft.

Mollie looked away. 'Besides, it's not as if a gardener was necessary when no one lived in the house and it was half falling down anyway. It was only Annabelle's charity that gave us a place to stay. We didn't need to be there.' She took a breath and let it out slowly. 'And you certainly don't need to pay us for the privilege.'

'I'm sorry if I insulted you by giving you the money,' Jacob said after a moment.

'It was very generous of you,' Mollie said quickly. 'I wasn't insulted.' She had been, bizarrely, hurt. As if money could fix the heartache and loneliness of those years. Write a cheque and be done with it.

'I'm sorry,' Jacob said quietly. 'I hurt more people than I even realised by leaving.' Mollie's heart twisted. For so many years she'd imagined Jacob leaving carelessly, without a thought or concern for the people he'd left behind. She'd seen Annabelle check the post every day for letters, and when none had come Mollie had assumed Jacob didn't care enough to write. She'd pictured him partying in some glamorous city, too involved in his own pleasure to think of his family or Wolfe Manor. She had, Mollie knew, tarred Jacob with the same brush as his father, and she knew now that wasn't fair.

Yet why *had* he left? How could he have done such an agonising thing, knowing the pain it would cause his family? She still didn't know him well enough to understand, or ask the question.

'It's okay,' she said now. 'It's time to move on.' She paused, then dared to add, 'For both of us.'

Jacob didn't reply.

They didn't speak for a while after that, and Mollie was glad. She'd much rather enjoy the day, as Jacob forewent the motorway for country lanes with their bright hedgerows, the fields dotted with primroses and buttercups, and the sun shone down benevolently upon them.

Mollie started to relax, the tension slipping away from her the farther they travelled from Wolfe Manor. Jacob seemed to relax as well, for his grip on the steering wheel loosened and he draped one arm along the back of the seat, so his fingers nearly brushed her shoulder.

Not that she should be so achingly aware of his nearness, Mollie told herself, or tempted to close that tiny distance. It would be so easy to shift in her seat so he was actually touching her—barely, but she knew she'd feel it. She'd feel it right down to her toes. Just the thought sent a blush firing her body. She was so amazingly, agonisingly aware of him, her body attuned to his in a way that was both pleasure and pain.

Despite this aching awareness the hours passed in a happy haze; it was so pleasant to be speeding along in a fancy car with a gorgeous man at the wheel. Mollie decided to enjoy the moment—and the whole weekend—for what it was. Something surreal, out of time, and certainly wonderful.

They arrived at the Grand Wolfe, and an officious-looking concierge showed them to their suite himself. Sebastian, he told Jacob, was out of town with his new wife, Aneesa.

Mollie noticed the speculative and envious looks a few women in the lobby slid her way, the respectful deference of the entire hotel staff towards Jacob. He strode through the lobby unaware of the admiration, yet clearly accepting of the respect. Mollie was suddenly conscious that Jacob was a *Wolfe*, the head of a noble English family, and she felt a swell of pride that she was on his arm.

Once in the hotel suite Mollie took in the set of elegant rooms, all of which looked to be equipped with every imaginable luxury. She peeked into an en suite bathroom that had a huge, sunken marble tub, glanced at the wide private terrace that could easily hold fifty people and marvelled at the living room with its plush sofas and hidden widescreen television; the concierge showed them how the painting that hid it folded back at the press of a button.

And of course she noticed the bedrooms—two of them—positioned at either end of a hallway so they could both have adequate privacy. Even so, the sight of the canopied king-size bed with its smooth, silken sheets made something in

her bump unsteadily, for there could be no question that this
luxury suite was also romantic.

Yet neither of them was here for romance.

'You can change if you like,' Jacob said once the concierge had left them alone. 'And then we can head off to the
expo.'

Mollie nodded. 'I'll freshen up and be right out.' She disappeared into the bedroom; her suitcase lay on a luggage
rack, already opened, her cocktail dress hanging in a huge
walnut wardrobe. Mollie hesitated, because she hadn't actually brought enough clothes to change after just a few
hours. Were you *supposed* to change on arrival at a place
like this? She had no idea. She'd never stayed in a hotel like
this before. The closest she'd come is when she'd splurged
on a *pensione* in Florence that actually had its own en suite
bathroom, a tiny cubicle with peeling lino and a leaky tap.

Shrugging this aside, Mollie pulled a brush through
her hair which had, of course, become unbearably tangled
during the drive. She washed her hands and face and re-
applied her lipstick, finishing off with a spritz of perfume.
She gazed at her reflection in the mirror with critical glum-
ness; her hair was still wild and her cheeks were pink from
the sun. So was her nose. She had more freckles than usual,
and if not for the fact that she was no longer gap-toothed she
could have passed for herself when she was eight years old,
going the entire summer with bare feet and skinned knees.

Sighing, she turned away from the mirror and slipped on
the fitted jacket she'd worn that first night Jacob had seen
her. She added a scarf in primrose yellow, deciding this con-
stituted enough of a wardrobe change, and headed back out
to the living room.

Jacob was opening a bottle of champagne as she came
into the room. 'Compliments of the hotel,' he said with a
flicker of a smile as he reached for two crystal flutes. 'I
thought we could toast the weekend.'

Mollie felt that unsteady bump inside again. She was afraid it was her heart. 'That sounds lovely,' she said, and took the proffered glass.

Jacob clinked his flute lightly with hers. 'To a change of scene,' he said, and Mollie nodded.

'Hear, hear.' She drank, and as she did she saw that Jacob's dark eyes were fixed on hers, and despite the apparent lightness of the moment his expression had turned brooding. So many hidden thoughts. So many unspoken memories.

She put her glass down on a side table and gave him a bright smile. 'Shall we?'

'Yes indeed.' Jacob set his glass down next to hers, and Mollie noticed that he hadn't drunk any of his champagne. Then she watched with relief as he smiled, the brooding expression replaced by something far lighter, and holding out his arm so Mollie could—all too naturally—slip hers into his, he led her from the room.

The expo was amazing. Even during her university days Mollie had seen nothing like it: display after display of architectural plans and blueprints, models of houses and buildings, gardens recreated in tiny, exquisite spaces, all innovative, unique and completely wondrous.

She wandered through the exhibition halls, Jacob at her side, her eyes as wide as a child's. Her mind buzzed with ideas of new techniques, hybrids and landscaping concepts, and she couldn't quite seem to help herself from sharing it all with Jacob.

'I've never seen an arrangement like that before.... There are so many new kinds of water features now.... Did you see the use of wildflowers in that exhibit? Most gardeners would consider them *weeds*....'

And Jacob listened, and made comments, and asked questions, so Mollie felt like he was genuinely interested. Like he genuinely cared.

Uh-oh. Don't go there, her mind warned. Don't start to believe some nonsense like he is interested in you...could *love* you....

Love was not a word she'd ever associate with Jacob Wolfe.

Yet as they strolled through the various displays and exhibitions, Mollie wondered what word she *would* associate with him. What kind of man was he? She'd assumed so much, and now she felt those assumptions were being swept away—yet replaced with what? Jacob never talked about himself, never offered any information or preferences or opinions. He was so self-controlled, so self-contained, that the man was practically a cipher.

Yet then she saw a flash of something in his eyes, something deep and dark and *raw*—and she knew there was far more to Jacob than she could ever imagine or understand.

While he was talking to some colleagues—they treated him with a wary, deferential respect—she perused the expo's programme, noting in its write-up the number of prestigious awards J Design had garnered.

> *J Design has always had the unique ability of creating a space with the individual needs of its client first in mind, so that the building takes on the characteristics of the client rather than the architect...*

Even in his business Jacob revealed nothing of himself. The omission, Mollie decided, was intentional. Jacob didn't reveal anything because he didn't want to be known.

Why?

He joined her again as she stood in front of a Japanese Zen garden, admiring the raked sand, the careful placement of stones and the little painted bridge that led into the tranquil scene.

Jacob gazed at it a moment with her before asking, 'What do you think?'

'It's very peaceful.'

'Yes, gardens are meant to be places of stillness and tranquillity in Eastern culture.' He pointed to an assortment of rocks that had been arranged off-centre. 'Nothing in a Zen garden is symmetrical, because according to their belief system nothing in life is.'

'Nothing in life is symmetrical?' Mollie asked, frowning slightly as she considered this.

'Nothing in life is perfect.' Jacob gave her the ghost of a smile. 'We must embrace the imperfections in the world as well as in ourselves in order to achieve peace or happiness.'

She turned to him. 'Do you believe that?'

'I try,' Jacob replied wryly. 'I have no trouble believing the world possesses imperfections,' he added. 'Or that they exist in myself. But to embrace them…' He trailed off, glancing at the garden with a frown, and Mollie wondered what he was thinking.

'You seem to know quite a bit about Zen gardens.'

'I spent some time in the East. My first building project was in Nepal.'

'Really?' Mollie had had no idea he'd travelled so far in his years away. She laid a hand on his arm. 'Thank you for taking me here, Jacob. It's been a wonderful experience.'

He turned to her with a smile. 'Yes, it has. I've enjoyed watching you take everything in.' Mollie blushed with pleasure at this admission. 'I'd like to take you out to dinner,' Jacob continued. 'As a way to finish a wonderful day. Did you bring anything to wear in the evening?'

Mollie's blush deepened. 'Yes,' she admitted, for the very fact that she had made her think he knew she'd been hoping there would be such an occasion to wear it.

'Good,' Jacob said briskly. 'Why don't we go back to the hotel and freshen up? Our reservation is for eight.'

* * *

Jacob prowled through the living room of the hotel suite as he waited for Mollie to finish dressing for dinner. He felt restless and edgy, and that numbing control he kept around him like a comforting blanket seemed to have slipped away completely.

Coming to London had been a bad idea. No, he corrected himself savagely, bringing Mollie to London had been a bad idea.

He'd enjoyed it too much.

Moodily Jacob gazed out at the cityscape laid out before him; the darkened streets twinkled with a steady stream of cars and taxis. He'd fully intended to keep his distance from Mollie; hadn't that been the point of his sordid little proposition?

Even if it had, Jacob could not pretend to himself that he'd been relieved when she'd rejected him. He'd been disappointed.

He'd wanted her. He wanted her still. He wanted her warmth and sweetness, found himself seeking the suddenness of her smile, the lightening of her eyes to amber, the barest brush of her skin, like warm silk. And while he'd told himself he'd brought Mollie to London for her own sake, so she could escape the confines of Wolfe Manor and actually enjoy herself, he knew he was a liar.

He'd brought her to London for his sake. His pleasure. He'd loved seeing Mollie looking so interested, so excited, so vibrant and alive. He'd loved sharing the sights of the expo with her, of hearing her talk and exchanging ideas and simply being together. He'd been alone for so long, contained, controlled, and yet when he was with Mollie, he didn't feel alone. He didn't feel lonely.

It would be so easy to get used to that feeling, to revel in the companionship, to surrender to the desire. For Jacob knew he didn't want just companionship; he wanted surrender. Sex, if he was going to be blunt. To bury himself

inside the yielding softness of her body, to lose himself in
the sweetness of her kiss. A chance to forget who he was
and what he'd done and maybe even find something new.
Something better.

And yet he knew that was impossible. There was nothing
new or better—not for him. And he couldn't bring Mollie
down with him, down into the darkness and chaos of his own
mind, the danger of his memories, and he knew he would if
he let himself get close to her. Care for her, and let her care
for him. Sex alone would accomplish it, for their relationship
had already moved past a soulless sexual bargain. It would
mean more to Mollie. It might even mean more to him. He
would sully her with his own sin, and the truth of who he
was—who he could become if he allowed himself the opportunity.

He'd already seen the darkness in himself, the darkness
that had caused his father's death and his family's fracture.
He couldn't bear for Mollie to see it.

Jacob swung away from the window, impatient with his
own maudlin musings. He'd had plenty of time to get used to
the darkness of his own soul. He lived with it the way others
lived with a more obvious handicap. Constant, endurable.
Just.

Yet in his bleaker moments he felt as if he were filled
with nothing *but* darkness; it seeped out through his eyes, his
pores. People felt it. He knew Mollie did; he'd seen her look
at him with a sad, puzzled frown, a little wrinkle of distress
marring her smooth forehead. And he knew he couldn't explain.

How did you tell someone about the blackness of your
soul? How did you admit the things you'd thought and done,
and how they tormented you still? How did you seek absolu-
tion from the one person who could never give it? Yourself.

He could never forgive himself for what he'd done. He'd
relived the moment of his father's death over and over; he

saw it night after night in his dreams. And while he knew that memories were faulty and dreams hardly reliable, what he remembered made him wonder. Doubt. What he remembered made him afraid…of himself.

'I'm ready.'

Jacob whirled around, blinking several times before he could focus properly on the vision in front of him. Mollie frowned.

'Jacob?' she said, hesitation in his name. 'Are you all right?'

Too late Jacob realised he was scowling ferociously, still in thrall to his memories. He made himself relax, felt his face soften into something close to a smile.

'Sorry, I was a million miles away.'

She took a step forward. 'It wasn't a nice place, wherever it was.'

'No,' Jacob agreed quietly. 'It wasn't.' He gazed down at her, taking in her slender frame swathed in lavender silk. 'You look beautiful, Mollie.' The dress clung to her curves and made his palms ache to touch her. She'd attempted to tame her wild curls into some sort of smooth chignon, and he could see the soft, vulnerable curve of her neck. Her skin was pale and covered with a shimmering of golden freckles. He wanted to touch his fingers to that hidden curve, brush it with his lips, feel its petal-softness as he had that night in the study. He took a step away.

Tonight was about control, not only of his body, but his mind. Jacob knew he would need every lesson he'd learned during his time in Nepal, every shred of experience and practice, in order to resist the greatest temptation he'd ever faced, far more than a whisky bottle or a clenched fist: the intoxicating sweetness of Mollie Parker.

CHAPTER SIX

'This is lovely.' Mollie gazed around at the restaurant on Park Lane with its heavy linen tablecloths and tinkling crystal glasses. The menu was so heavy she'd laid it in her lap, and when the waiter had brought a basket of rolls she'd actually dropped hers on the floor.

She felt completely out of her element, inexperienced, nervous, ridiculous. She'd seen the looks women had given Jacob, lascivious and full of longing. Then they'd looked at her, incredulous and envious, and Mollie knew they were wondering what she could possibly be doing with Jacob Wolfe. She was wondering the same thing. The gardener's daughter and the lord's son, and she had an awful, horrible feeling that Jacob was taking her out tonight simply out of pity. Perhaps that was what the whole weekend had been about: a mercy mission.

'Do you think so?' Jacob asked, and he sounded amused. 'Because you're frowning quite ferociously at the moment.'

'Am I?' Mollie felt herself add a flush to the frown and she suppressed a groan. 'Well, if I am, it's only because I dropped my roll and I hate doing things like that.' If she couldn't be sophisticated, she might as well be honest.

'You're frowning that much over a roll?' Jacob said, and he sounded even more amused.

'It's not the roll,' she explained. 'It's the fact that I've never been in a restaurant like this, or had a weekend like this, while you've been sipping champagne out of a silk slipper your whole life!'

Jacob said nothing for a moment. He went still, as Mollie knew he always did. It made him utterly inscrutable—and annoying.

'Sipping champagne out of a silk slipper,' he repeated musingly. 'Now, I'm quite sure that's something I've never done.'

'Because you don't drink champagne,' Mollie returned, the words slipping out before she could stop them. 'Do you?'

'No, I don't,' Jacob confirmed quietly. Mollie gestured towards his untouched glass.

'And you're not going to drink that, are you?'

'No.'

'Why did you pour it, then?' Curiosity, a need to understand Jacob, drove her to the demanding questions.

Jacob hesitated for a single second. 'Because I didn't want you to feel uncomfortable,' he finally said, and colour rushed once more into Mollie's face.

'Oh.' She lapsed into silence, and Jacob reached across the table to lightly lay his hand across hers. Despite the gentleness of the touch, Mollie started as if he'd just prodded her with a live wire. The warmth of his hand covering hers flooded through her body, made heat pool deep inside of her.

'Mollie, what's wrong?'

Mollie looked at him; all the harsh remoteness had softened into an expression that was both serious and sorrowful, and a sudden, inexplicable lump rose in her throat so she could barely speak.

'I don't know. I suppose I'm a bit…self-conscious. We're so different.'

'That's not a bad thing,' Jacob said quietly, and suddenly Mollie's discomfort about the difference in their life experiences seemed ridiculous—and unimportant.

'Don't say that,' she said, leaning towards him. 'It's not true.'

'You don't know what's true,' Jacob said, his voice light, although his eyes looked dark, blacker than ever.

'Then tell me,' Mollie said, imploring, and Jacob just shook his head.

'Hardly dinner table conversation.'

Mollie suppressed a sigh of exasperation. 'I don't mean who we are as people anyway. I mean class.' There. She'd said it.

'*Class?*' Jacob repeated in blatant disbelief. He sat back in his chair, folding his arms, one eyebrow arched. He was so clearly sceptical that he made her feel as if she were living in the pages of a Victorian novel while he had a wholly modern outlook on life.

'Yes, class, Jacob,' she replied a bit tartly. 'And it's been my experience that people in the upper classes don't think such a thing exists.'

'Mollie, we're living in the twenty-first century. Class constructs are irrelevant.'

'Maybe to you, but they're not to me. Not when all this—' She swept out an arm to encompass the restaurant, the hotel, his world, and knocked over her water glass. It clattered to the floor with an almighty crash, the crystal shattering into dangerous-looking shards. 'Oh.' Mollie bit her lip, mortified. She looked up to see Jacob observing her calmly, completely unruffled by her undignified display. 'I think,' she said, 'I just illustrated my point perfectly.'

And then Jacob did something she'd never seen or heard him do: he laughed. The sound startled her; it wasn't dry or mocking or cold. It was a pure, joyous peal that rang clear through her, and made her smile and then laugh as well, despite her initial embarrassment.

'Oh, Mollie,' Jacob said, leaning over to clasp her hand with his once more, his fingers curling warmly around hers, 'whatever differences there are between us, I wouldn't change a thing about you. Not one blessed thing.'

And with his hand still on hers and his laugh still echoing in her ears, Mollie thought she wouldn't change anything at that moment either.

A waiter had hurried to clean up the mess, and within seconds he'd whisked the shattered crystal away and replaced Mollie's glass on the table. Jacob sat back, slipping his hands from hers, and his expression cleared so it was almost as if that wondrous moment of shared laughter had never been.

Mollie gazed down at her menu. She didn't know why she'd brought up the class differences between them. Jacob was right, they were irrelevant. She had a gnawing suspicion that her complaint had really been just a cover for what she really felt: fear. Fear that she was starting to care for Jacob. Fear of what might happen if she let herself fall all the way. It wouldn't, perhaps, be that great a distance.

'Now *you* look a million miles away,' Jacob said quietly, and Mollie looked up, trying to smile.

'I suppose I was. But never mind.' She pushed the thoughts away and tried to smile.

'Mollie…?' Jacob prompted gently. A smile quirked the corner of his mouth. 'Tell me the most wonderful thing you saw today.'

And filled with a sudden, buoyant relief at having an excuse *not* to think or fear, Mollie did.

The rest of the dinner conversation flowed smoothly, surprisingly so, for as Mollie let all those prickly concerns and doubts slip away for a little while, she found Jacob wonderfully easy to talk to. He listened with that grave stillness she'd come to appreciate, and yet after an hour when several courses had been cleared and she was toying with the last of her chocolate mousse gateau, she realised she'd been talking about herself the whole time; Jacob hadn't said anything. Shared anything.

'I must be boring you,' she said with a little laugh. 'Talking so much.' She placed her fork on a plate with a clatter.

'Not at all.'

'Tell me something about yourself.' Jacob said nothing, and Mollie thought what an appropriate response that was. 'Tell me about Nepal,' she said.

He gave a little shrug. 'What do you want to know?'

'What made you go there? What did you do there? What was it like?' She propped her chin in her hands and gave him a teasing smile. 'I've never travelled, except for my one trip to Italy. Tell me everything.' Jacob hesitated, and Mollie felt as if she'd just asked him to extract his eyeteeth and hand them to her. 'Why is it so difficult to talk about it?' she asked softly, and he gave her the glimmer of a smile.

'I told you, I've been a very private man.'

'I'm not asking you to spill state secrets, am I?' Mollie said. She kept her voice light, her smile mischievous. Yet even so, she found herself asking something she knew instinctively was far too personal. 'Why have you been so private? What are you trying to hide?'

Jacob stilled, stiffened. Mollie realised she might have offended him. She bit her lip, then opened her mouth to utter a hasty apology, when Jacob spoke first. 'Everything.' He spoke the word lightly, almost as a joke, yet one look into those fathomlessly black eyes, and Mollie knew it wasn't.

She knew it was the stark, literal truth, and it made her ache with a nameless sorrow. She could only imagine how it made Jacob feel.

'Well, then,' she said after a moment, 'let's keep it about Nepal. Did you go to Kathmandu? Did you see the Dalai Lama? Oh, that's Tibet, isn't it?'

He laughed lightly. 'Yes, it is. I didn't see him, I'm afraid. But I did spend some time in a monastery.'

'Really?' Intrigued, she leaned forward. 'Why? I mean... it's not exactly a usual holiday destination, is it?'

'I wasn't on a holiday. I worked my way across Europe and Asia, and ended up in Nepal. I stayed in a small village that had been devastated by flooding from the local river, and so I helped them to rebuild.' He gave her a small smile. 'My first building project.'

'And then?' Mollie asked. She loved hearing about him, about what he'd done.

'I kept working.' His hand, lying loosely on the tabletop, tightened briefly. 'As much as I could. When I worked, I didn't have to think. Or sleep.'

'Sleep?' Mollie repeated. 'Why didn't you want to sleep?'

Jacob shrugged, and Mollie could tell he regretted what he'd said. 'I just enjoyed working,' he replied in a tone of unmistakable dismissal. 'Seeing something being built, made good.' He took a sip of water. 'Anyway, I worked too much and ended up becoming quite ill with a fever. The villagers took me to the nearest monastery to recover, and I stayed there for several months, getting stronger and learning from the monks.'

'What did you learn?'

'Control, over the mind as well as the body.' He paused, his fingers toying with the stem of his water glass. 'Control is crucial.'

Mollie said nothing. What was Jacob trying to control? What part of himself needed such a stern hand? The man she'd come to know was kind, thoughtful, thinking of others before himself. Yet by the harsh light in Jacob's eyes, Mollie knew he didn't see himself that way...the way she did.

'Well,' she finally said in an effort to break the silence, 'it sounds fascinating, even if you didn't get to Kathmandu.'

Jacob looked up, a smile now quirking the corner of his mouth. 'Maybe next time.'

'Next time,' Mollie agreed, and then they both lapsed into

a silence that seemed suddenly heavy with tense expectation. Mollie was achingly conscious that they were in a beautiful restaurant, having eaten a wonderful meal, and that in just about every way this evening should have been a date. Surely people thought they were on a date, lingering over the last crumbs of their dessert, gazing into each other's eyes?

She realised she wanted it to be a date; she wanted Jacob to smile lazily and say—

'Care to dance?'

Mollie stiffened in surprise. She had no idea if Jacob had said that or if she had just imagined it, fantasised she'd heard it because she wanted it so much.

'Pardon?'

Jacob smiled, gesturing towards the jazz band that was playing a slow, sensual tune in the corner of the restaurant.

'Do you want to dance?'

Mollie swallowed. Jacob had asked lightly, as if it meant nothing, but she could see that dark, intense gleam in his eyes and knew how dangerous it would be to let herself glide in his arms.

How much she wanted it.

'Okay,' she said, her voice no more than a whisper, and then wordlessly she took Jacob's outstretched hand and rose from the table, following him onto the dance floor.

Control was crucial. So he'd said.

As Jacob slid his arms around Mollie's slender waist, he felt his control stretching to a single frayed thread. He shouldn't have asked her to dance. He shouldn't have tempted himself so far, knowing how he could break. Want.

Hurt.

He closed his eyes, drawing her closer, inhaling the sweetness of her hair, something between lilac and soap. She smelled clean. Fresh. Pure.

He felt her hesitation; it travelled through her body in a

FREE Merchandise is 'in the Cards' for you!

Dear Reader,

We're giving away FREE MERCHANDISE!

Seriously, we'd like to reward you for reading this novel by giving you **FREE MERCHANDISE** worth over **$20**. And no purchase is necessary!

You see the Jack of Hearts sticker above? Paste that sticker in the box on the Free Merchandise Voucher inside. Return the Voucher promptly...and we'll send you valuable Free Merchandise!

Thanks again for reading one of our novels—and enjoy your Free Merchandise with our compliments!

Pam Powers

Pam Powers

P.S. Look inside to see what Free Merchandise is **"in the cards"** for you!

H-P-02/12

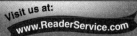

YOUR FREE MERCHANDISE INCLUDES...

2 FREE Harlequin Presents® Books
AND 2 FREE Mystery Gifts

FREE MERCHANDISE VOUCHER

2 FREE
BOOKS
and
2 FREE
GIFTS

Please send my Free Merchandise, consisting of
2 Free Books and **2 Free Mystery Gifts**.
I understand that I am under no obligation to buy
anything, as explained on the back of this card.

❏ I prefer the regular-print edition
106/306 HDL FMNH

❏ I prefer the larger-print edition
176/376 HDL FMNH

Please Print

FIRST NAME

LAST NAME

ADDRESS

APT.#   CITY

STATE/PROV.   ZIP/POSTAL CODE

NO PURCHASE NECESSARY!

The Reader Service - Here's how it works:

trembling wave and then she relaxed into him, her breasts brushing his chest, her hair his cheek in a silken whisper. He heard her give a small, soft sigh, and he knew she'd surrendered to the dance, to him.

If he wanted her, he could have her. He could take her upstairs and strip that lavender dress from her slowly, let it pool at her feet and then take her for his own. Obliterate his own wretched self in the soft yielding of her body. She wouldn't resist. Wouldn't be able to, for she felt that treacherous tug of desire as much as he did.

It would be so easy. So wonderful. So *wrong*.

Jacob closed his eyes and tried to summon his control. His strength. He needed it now more than ever, for he couldn't do what he wanted. He knew that, had accepted it. The women he'd taken to his bed had always been as worldly and jaded as he was, perfectly willing to accept his soulless conditions. Sex was a transaction, mutually satisfying, emotionally barren. No chance of anyone being hurt...by him. He had nothing to give—nothing worthwhile—and he wanted nothing in return.

Yet now he wanted. He wanted Mollie in ways he'd never wanted a woman. Not just in his arms, but in his thoughts. His head. Even his heart. He'd enjoyed talking with her, had wanted to tell her more. He'd felt her interest and her sympathy touch a dark, raw place inside of him that no one ever saw.

When Mollie asked him questions, he wanted to answer. He wanted to brush the curl that lay against her cheek and kiss her sweet mouth, already puckered into a thoughtful frown. He wanted to smooth her forehead and brush his lips against the freckles that shimmered across her shoulders. He wanted all of her, body and mind and perhaps even soul and heart, and that thought terrified him more than the worst nightmare he'd ever had.

For what came after, what would surely happen if he gave

in to such desire, was perhaps worse than what he'd already done. He'd accepted that he'd hurt his siblings by leaving, had made peace with it because the decision had been so necessary, so absolute.

He couldn't accept hurting Mollie, which would surely happen if he stayed with her. Loved her. Eventually his true self would be revealed, just as it had been the night he'd raised his hand to his father. The night he'd ended one misery, and embarked on another. He would never be free. You couldn't be free of yourself.

Control. Jacob instinctively tightened his grip around Mollie, pulled her closer still. He didn't want to let her go. One dance. One dance in a public place was safe enough. He could give himself that.

And then…then he would walk away. Just as he always did.

They didn't speak. Mollie knew words would break what was growing and stretching between them, this silent, sensuous dance that was still edged with desperation. She felt it when Jacob pulled her closer, she recognised it in herself. She didn't want it to end.

She laid her cheek against Jacob's shoulder and breathed in the scent of him, the faint tang of his aftershave, the warm musk that was simply him. She felt him stiffen slightly in surprise, and then his fingers splayed along the curve of her hips so that she was pressed against him from shoulder to thigh.

When he touched his finger to her chin and tipped her face upwards, it seemed utterly natural and right for Mollie to let him do so, to wait, her eyes half closed, her lips parted for him to kiss her. She knew, at least in one fuzzy part of her brain, that she was offering herself in a silent, yearning invitation. She recognised that, and didn't care. Shame and pride had ceased to matter or even exist.

There was only this moment, silent, wonderful, *hopeful*, and yet…

He didn't kiss her.

His finger still touched her chin, cool and dry, and Mollie opened her eyes to find him gazing down at her with such an expression of conflicted torment that she gasped involuntarily.

'Jacob…' she whispered, just as she had once before, when just as now he'd touched her with one finger and looked at her with such pain. What kept him from kissing her? Was even this about control?

The word died on her lips as he bent his head and finally closed the distance between their lips as she'd so wanted him to. He stole the very breath from her as his lips touched hers, moving over her mouth as if exploring this new, precious territory. Then he deepened the kiss, pulling her even closer so their bodies felt joined, seamless, and desire plunged deep in her belly; her hands fisted in his hair, awareness of anything but Jacob and the desperate sweetness of his kiss fading to nothing.

For it *was* desperate. The kiss was imbued with a longing that made Mollie feel like this was all they would have, all Jacob would allow, and she pressed closer, wanting more. Asking for more.

Jacob broke the kiss, his breath a raw shudder. 'It's late,' he said. His voice sounded hoarse and he stepped away quickly, leaving Mollie half stumbling in the remnants of a dance. She gathered herself quickly, straightening her shoulders and nodding even though her breath came in gasps and her lips stung from his kiss.

She didn't dare speak, couldn't, as she followed Jacob from the dance floor. He walked stiffly, his body radiating a new tension.

They didn't speak all the way up to the hotel suite. Mollie

felt unbearably flat. There was no heady expectation, no sensual tension.

Mollie didn't know why Jacob had stopped, why he'd felt he had to stop. So much for his proposition. He must have known she would have accepted tonight—and yet he'd refused. For that was what the ending of that kiss felt like: a refusal. A rejection. And why? He wanted her; she knew that. She'd felt that. Yet something—some memory, perhaps—kept Jacob from acting on his instincts, fulfilling his desires. And perhaps it was for the better, because if anything happened between them it would surely end up causing her pain.

Even if, for a moment, for a night, it would be so very sweet.

Still silent, Mollie followed Jacob into the suite. In their absence the staff had tidied up and left a few low lamps burning, so the huge space seemed cosy and intimate.

Jacob ignored it all, ignored her, as he crossed the living room to his bedroom at the end of the hall.

'Good night,' he said, without even turning around.

Mollie retreated into her own bedroom; the sheets had been turned down, a silk robe laid out on the end of the bed. She touched its luxurious softness briefly, sighing again, amazed at how unhappy she felt when the evening, the whole day, had been so wonderful.

It was only a little past ten o'clock, yet the evening was already over. Reluctantly Mollie slipped off her dress and reached for her pyjamas. She didn't feel remotely tired; her mind and body still fizzed and ached, and she knew it would be hours before she could sleep.

Hours to think and remember and *want*.

She stretched out on the bed, too restless even to close her eyes. What was keeping her from leaving her bedroom right now, and going to Jacob? Telling him she'd accept his no-strings suggestion?

I never should have suggested such a thing.

Would he reject her if she actually came to him, told him what she wanted? Showed him, even? Could she risk it?

And, the far more important question was, if he didn't turn away, if he accepted her offer, could she risk *that*?

There was only one way to find out.

Abruptly Mollie sat up. She'd lived life on the sides and in the shadows for too long: most of her childhood, most of her adult life. There had been a few sweet years in university when she'd felt a part of things, happy and *normal*, but the rest of her life had been cloaked in isolation.

No more. She was tired of it, tired of the loneliness. She wanted to live. She wanted Jacob.

Quickly, before she lost courage, Mollie threw off her pyjamas. She could hardly seduce Jacob in nubby fleece, yet she wasn't quite bold enough to go stark naked. She put on her silk dress instead; she felt beautiful in it, and she needed that boost.

Then, taking a deep breath, she opened her door and headed out into the darkened hallway.

The entire suite was bathed in silence, and she could hear the steady ticking of the clock—or was that her heart? Letting out a little breath of laughter, Mollie pressed her hand against her wildly beating heart, far faster than the clock. Heaven help her, she was so nervous.

She tiptoed along the hallway towards Jacob's forbiddingly closed door; no light shone from underneath. Maybe he was asleep. Maybe he had no reason to feel restless and edgy and aching, the way she did. Maybe she'd imagined it all. Mollie hesitated for a second, her hand hovering over the doorknob. Then, possessed by both a boldness and a courage she'd never known she had, she turned the knob and, with another deep breath, pushed the door open.

The bedroom was empty.

Mollie felt it before she saw it; it took a few moments for

her eyes to accustom to the darkness. At least the hallway
had been lit from the lamp left on in the living room.

The room *felt* empty, the door to the dark en suite bathroom ajar, and Mollie saw the bed was untouched.

Jacob had gone.

This was the test: a tumbler of whisky, glinting under the low
lights from the bar. Jacob placed it in front of him and folded
his arms. Then he waited.

He hadn't performed this test in years, for it had become
too easy. He needed greater challenges, bigger proofs of his
self-control.

I am not that man.

Yet now he'd been reduced to what he always feared: that
he *was* that man, the man his father had been, the man he'd
shown himself to be when he'd lost control that terrible evening…no matter what the justification. He was just like his
father.

No. He could conquer that impulse, control it. He had to,
because if he didn't—? What then? He would be no better
than his father. No better than the boy who had placed his fist
in his father's face with so many years of pent-up rage, who
had raised his hand to his own precious sister in a moment
of anger.

He *was* that man.

Yet when he performed these tests, and succeeded, he felt,
at least for a moment, that he wasn't. Tonight he needed an
easy victory. God only knew walking away from Mollie—
from her mouth and her eyes and the sweet scent of her
hair—had been far too hard.

Yet victory, tonight, did not come easily. He stared at the
tumbler of whisky for twenty minutes. Once he reached for
it. His hand trembled and he was appalled. He hadn't reached
for the glass in years. A decade, at least. He jerked his hand

back, folding his arms so his fingers curled around his biceps hard enough to hurt.

He was so weak.

'You going to drink that?' The bartender glanced rather sourly at the untouched glass; undoubtedly he'd been hoping for a more lucrative barfly. Jacob smiled tightly.

'Leave it.'

Shrugging, the bartender turned away. It was only a little past eleven, but Jacob was the only customer in the hotel bar. This wasn't the kind of place to encourage drunks to order another round. Everyone else had retired to their far more comfortable hotel rooms.

Jacob knew he couldn't go there. Not when Mollie would be so close, maybe even waiting. He'd fail that test for sure.

'Jacob...?'

Jacob stiffened. He turned slowly to see Mollie standing in the entrance to the bar. She still wore her beautiful dress, but her hair was wild and unruly, her face pale and shocked. He could see the freckles standing in bold relief on her nose.

He almost reached for the whisky again.

He curled his fingers tighter, his nails biting into his own flesh, and nodded tersely, feeling something close to resignation. There would always be a test he could not pass. A way to fail.

'Hello, Mollie.'

CHAPTER SEVEN

MOLLIE stepped into the bar, amazed to find Jacob there. She'd been wandering through the hotel, down empty corridors, disconsolate, uncertain, wondering where he'd gone, *why* he'd gone.

And then she'd found him here.

Cautiously she slipped onto the stool next to him and nodded towards the tumbler. 'You aren't going to drink that, are you?'

'No.'

'Why?' she asked softly. There were so many whys: why was he here, why did he look so conflicted, why didn't he want to kiss her any more? She left it simply at *Why?* and let Jacob choose which one to answer.

'The point,' he said carefully, his tone clinical and even a bit cold, 'is *not* to drink it.'

'Why?' Mollie asked again.

Jacob paused. He smiled, and it looked brittle, fragile. Like his whole face, his whole self, might splinter apart. 'It's a test,' he said simply. 'How long can I sit here without touching it.'

'You've been here a while already,' Mollie said quietly. 'How long do you intend to torture yourself, Jacob?'

He laughed rawly. 'You have no idea.'

'No, I don't,' she whispered. 'Tell me.' Jacob shook his head, the movement no more than an unsteady jerk. 'Is it because of your father? Are you worried you might have the same problem with alcohol that he did?'

'Alcohol is the least of it.'

She laid a hand on his arm. 'What happened?'

'Annabelle never told you?'

The question startled her. *Annabelle?* 'No...' Mollie felt as if she were spinning in a void of uncertainty, a world of ignorance. There were so many things she didn't know.

Jacob drew in a shuddering breath. 'After my father died—after I killed him—'

'Don't—'

'It's the truth, isn't it?' Jacob smiled grimly. 'Never apologise for the truth.' He lowered his head, his hand lying on the table now, a grasping fist, closer to the tumbler. 'You *can't.*'

'It was an accident, Jacob,' Mollie said firmly. 'And you were protecting Annabelle. Everyone knows that. You did the right thing....'

'And I didn't protect her, did I? Everyone can see the scars.'

What about your scars? Mollie wanted to ask. Who sees them? They were all on the inside, and for so long she'd had no idea they existed at all. How could she have assumed that Jacob had left all those years ago without a care in the world, selfish, self-centred? How could she have judged him so utterly? Yet she had, and his siblings had as well. Everyone had.

Especially himself.

'It doesn't matter,' he said roughly. He pulled his hand away from the bar. 'The point is I failed—just as my father failed.'

'No—'

'The day I left, Annabelle found me in my father's study. It was noon and I was already half drunk on his whisky.' He spoke with revulsion, but Mollie refused to give in to it.

'And so one moment of weakness condemns you, nearly twenty years later? I don't believe that, Jacob.'

'There's a lot you don't know,' he told her in a low voice.

'I'm sure there is. There's a lot you don't know about me too. One morning when my father was ill, he couldn't remember anything. Not my name, not that my mother had died decades ago. He was confused and scared and he started to cry.' She drew a breath, the memory still shaming her. 'And I yelled at him. I yelled at him like he was a naughty child. As if he could help it.' Her voice trembled. 'I'm ashamed of that.'

'You shouldn't be ashamed.' Jacob's voice was low. 'You stayed, Mollie. You saw it through.'

'And you blame yourself because you didn't stay?'

'No. I blame myself because I *couldn't*.' Jacob drew a shuddering breath. 'If I did...' He stopped, shaking his head, closing himself off. Mollie wouldn't let him.

'Our mistakes don't define us, Jacob.'

Jacob's voice was so low she could barely hear it. 'This is more than a mistake. This is who I am.'

The raw grief in his voice shook her. Why did he think so badly of himself? What was he not telling her? 'You're the boy who took care of his family, Jacob,' she said firmly. 'The man who saved his sister....'

Jacob shook his head, the movement violent and instinctive. 'You don't *know*—'

'No, I don't. I never could. I know your whole family suffered under William's hand, although I'm sure I could never guess how much. And,' she added softly, 'I'm sure, as the oldest, you endured the most of all.'

'It's not that.'

'Why do you carry so much guilt, Jacob?' Mollie asked softly. 'Why is it all your fault?'

'Because...' He stopped, shaking his head.

'Tell me.'

'No!' The word was a roar. He dropped his head in his hands, his fingers raking through his hair. 'I can't. If I told you...'

'What? What would happen?'

'You might hate me.' His voice dropped to a whisper. 'I couldn't bear that.'

Stunned and humbled, Mollie remained silent. Then she acted out of both instinct and a newborn confidence. She reached out to draw Jacob's hands away from his face, his head still bowed. He lifted it as she took his hands in hers, curling her fingers around his as she half slid off her stool to do what she'd wanted to do for so long, what she needed to do.

She kissed him.

Jacob's lips slackened under hers in surprise for a single second before he responded, his arms coming around Mollie's shoulders and drawing her closer to him so she leaned against him, half sprawled on his stool.

He kissed her with a pent-up passion that felt like fury and yet tasted so achingly sweet. *He* tasted sweet, and as she surrendered to the kiss he'd made his own she knew she would never get enough.

He pulled away for a brief, aching moment and shook his head. 'Not here.'

Mollie nodded, accepting, and then he took her hand and pulled her with him away from the bar, flinging a few crumpled notes on its polished surface. She followed him across the hotel's opulent lobby towards a gleaming bank of lifts; trepidation curled in the pit of her stomach. She was afraid this silent walk would give Jacob space and time to change his mind. To decide he didn't want her after all.

He jabbed the lift button and the doors swished open. The moment they closed again, Jacob turned to her, pulling her into his arms and kissing her with an abandoned hunger that thrilled Mollie to her core.

She responded, every inhibition and uncertainty scattering to the winds as she tangled her fingers in Jacob's hair and pressed her body against his, wanting and needing to feel all of him. Wanting and needing this, only this, this moment, this kiss—it was everything, her whole world wrapped into one embrace.

They stumbled back against the wall of the lift, fingers scrabbling at each other's clothes, their breathing ragged and desperate and yet the kiss went on, urgent, endless, demanding and satisfying at the same time. Jacob's hand pulled at the zip of her dress and he tugged impatiently; in one slithering movement it fell to the floor of the lift. Mollie kicked it off, pulling at the buttons of his shirt and hearing them pop and scatter across the floor as the lift began to slow.

She could hardly believe she was being this daring, this reckless; she was in a hotel lift in nothing but her bra and panties. And Jacob...to have him so urgent, so hungry. He was losing control, and it thrilled her.

He pulled her towards him, kissing her again with that same deep urgency. The doors whooshed open and in one easy movement Jacob scooped her into his arms and carried her into their suite.

He brought her to the bed, laying her gently down before he reached for the buttons of his shirt, most of which she'd already wrenched apart. Mollie watched him undress with desire-dazed eyes; he was so beautiful. He shrugged out of his shirt, the muscles of his shoulders and chest rippling with the simple movement. His hair was rumpled, his breathing ragged, and his eyes—

Oh, his eyes. There was so much pain in those black, black eyes, it made Mollie want to weep. She lay there, her mind still fogged with desire, and yet the pain she saw reached out to her and wrapped around her throat. Her heart. She could barely speak, barely breathe, so she just held her arms out to him in silent supplication.

He came to her.

He fell upon her with a hunger and a need Mollie hadn't expected, even now. It humbled her, excited her, made her feel sexy and beautiful and, God help her, even loved.

He buried his face in the curve of her neck, his hands roaming over her body, down to her stomach, his fingers skimming across the tender flesh of her inner thighs. She gasped under his touch; it had been so *long*. It had been for ever, because it had never been like this before.

'Mollie…' Her name sounded like a plea, and she rose to answer it.

'*Yes.*' She didn't want his doubt. She was sure, so very sure, and she wanted him to be as well. She held his head between her palms, dragging him forward so she could kiss him, as if her kiss was a balm she was bestowing upon him to take that pain from his eyes. From his heart.

And he accepted it, the tension leaving his body as he kissed her again, this time with a new, slow languor, a kiss to savour. He bent his head to her breasts, taking his turn with each, as Mollie gasped at the exquisite sensation. She felt Jacob smile against her skin, and then he moved lower. He covered every inch of her body, moving over her with his lips and hands, testing and tasting, treasuring her. Mollie arched beneath him, her voice a restless plea as the ache within her intensified, demanding release.

Finally he rolled on top of her, and Mollie welcomed his weight, eager for the joining of their bodies. She started in surprise as she felt Jacob touch her closed eyelids. 'Look at me.'

Her eyes fluttered open. 'Jacob…?'

'Look at me,' he said again as he entered her, filling her to completion, the moment of union so surprisingly, stingingly sweet that she had to blink sudden tears. Jacob braced himself on his forearms as he looked down at her, his eyes still so dark, his forehead furrowed. Silently he brushed the trace of a tear from the corner of her eye, and Mollie let out a gasping cry.

'It's all right....'

It was more than all right; it was wonderful. She felt consumed, filled, *whole*. And as her body spiralled into a climax, with Jacob still gazing at her with such heartfelt solemnity, she felt that this was what it was to be known. And Jacob felt it too. No matter what questions or secrets lay between them, he *knew* her.

And she knew him.

Then the thought—all her thoughts—splintered apart as her body convulsed around him and she cried out in a pleasure so sweetly intense it felt almost akin to pain. Jacob buried his face in her neck as he found his own release, and moments later, their bodies still slick with sweat, he rolled off her, one arm thrown over his eyes.

What had just happened?

She lay there, naked, a little cold, conscious of him next to her, silent save for the ragged tear of his breathing. She rolled towards him, placed a hand lightly on the ridged muscles of his taut stomach. She couldn't see his face. He placed his hand on hers, and Mollie's insides lurched with disappointment as he made to push it away. Then, to her surprise, he stilled. After a second's hesitation his fingers curled around hers and he kept her hand there, wrapped in his. They lay together, holding hands, not speaking, until, exhausted, Mollie eventually fell asleep.

Jacob listened to Mollie's breathing slow as she relaxed into sleep. From the corner of his eye he could see the brightness of her hair against the pillow, the soft, smooth curve of her cheek. She let out a satisfied little sigh and everything in Jacob clenched.

What had he just done? Where was his control *now*?

He let out a ragged sigh and raked a hand through his

sweat-dampened hair. His body felt good, satisfied and re-
plete in a way he'd never experienced before, but his mind
screamed and seethed in an agony of remorse. He'd done—
again—what he'd sworn he wouldn't do. He'd hurt someone. He'd hurt Mollie...or at least he would, when he let her
down. When she discovered just what kind of man he really
was.

You're not that man.

Carefully Jacob shifted on his side so he could look at her.
He kept her hand clasped in his, needing her touch even now.
She was curled on her side, her mouth softened in a smile,
her chest rising and falling gently in her sleep.

She was so beautiful. So innocent. So *good.*

How could he have seduced her? How could he have re-
sisted her?

Restless yet not wanting to disturb her, Jacob slipped from
the bed. Mollie's fingers clenched around his as he attempted
to extricate his hand from hers; gently he laid it palm up on
the sheets. He reached for his boxers and shrugged them
on, then stalked to the darkened privacy of the suite's living
room.

He stood in the centre of the room, listening to the distant noise of traffic, the relentless beat of his own heart.
Corrosive guilt poured through his craven heart, seeped into
its many cracks. He closed his eyes.

He should have left her alone. He shouldn't have touched
her, taken her, dragged her down with him. For surely that
was what he would do, if she ever knew. If he ever told her...

Suddenly Jacob opened his eyes. He stared unseeingly
out at the twinkling lights of the city below him, his own
thoughts reverberating through him.

If he told her.

What would happen?

What would happen if he told Mollie the truth of that

night, if he admitted to her the fears that lurked inside of him? If he told her just how like his father he really was?

It was a question Jacob had never asked himself. He'd never dared. It was too terrifying, too dangerous, to even think of telling anyone about the darkness inside him. Yet now, with the rush of damaging emotions coursing through him—regret, guilt, fear—he felt the faint life-giving trickle of another emotion he'd forgotten about, for he hadn't felt it in so long.

Hope.

What would happen if he told Mollie everything? If he gave her—*them*—a chance? A chance at what? His mind scoffed. After everything, what was he capable of? What did he have left to give?

Jacob knew he couldn't answer that. Not yet. But he would never get the chance to answer it if he didn't do the first: tell Mollie. Tell her everything.

His heart raced and his hands trembled as he paced the living room, stalking its corners as if it were the prison of his heart. He felt more restless than ever, anxious and uncertain and yet still pulsing with the faint heartbeat of hope.

He could do it. He could tell her, risk her knowing. Risk her rejection, even her revulsion. What did he really have to lose?

He'd lost everything already.

Even so, the thought of being honest with someone who already mattered so much to him was an unwelcome thought. A terrifying one. It would be so much easier, safer, to stay the way he was.

Alone.

Yet Jacob knew he was so utterly tired of being alone, exhausted by loneliness. He'd lived the past twenty years of his life as a restless workaholic, a wandering nomad who made acquaintances and lovers, yet no friends. No love.

He could hardly believe he was contemplating changing that. Risking it.

Yet with Mollie…

Why do you carry so much guilt, Jacob? Why is it all your fault?

He could risk it with her. He needed to take the risk, because God only knew he couldn't take much more of the life he had. He wanted more. He wanted the risk.

He wanted Mollie.

Jacob drew in a deep breath and let it out again in a slow shudder. Resolute and yet at peace, he turned back to the bedroom.

Mollie still lay curled on one side of the bed, her hand resting palm open where he'd left it. She let out another soft little sigh. Jacob slid into bed next to her. In her sleep Mollie curved into him, so it was utterly natural—utterly right—to take her into his arms, to fit her warm body against his. She nestled naturally into him, and she reached for his hand, her fingers threading through his.

Their bodies *fitted*.

Resting his chin on the softness of her hair, Jacob closed his eyes and slept.

The dream came for him that night. Of course it did; in his greedy hope he had made himself vulnerable. Always, always it was the same, except this time it was worse. *He* was worse.

It came to him in a red mist of rage. It was as if he saw everything—Annabelle, William, his younger brothers—through a hazy scarlet curtain. The house was dark all around him; Annabelle huddled on the floor, her knees drawn to her chest, her face already covered in blood. She was still, silent, although he heard his younger brothers' broken pleas to *Stop, please stop, Dad.*

His father didn't stop. William Wolfe's hand was raised,

the riding crop curled around his fist, his face twisted in a
terrible anger.

Jacob saw the whip, the blood, and he felt something in
him snap; it was as if he heard the sound deep within, the
very core of him crumbling under. *Too much.* It was finally,
finally too much.

Acting out of instinct, he pushed his father hard on the
shoulder, felt the flat of his palm connect with slack muscle.
He felt his own strength and his father's weakness. Then
William let out a bellow of rage, and he hit Annabelle again,
the crop slicing through the air and whistling as it connected
with her bloody flesh.

Jacob's fists clenched; he felt powerful with fury. He
felt like he could do anything, he *would* do anything in that
moment, to save his sister. To hurt his father. He heard the
deadly venom of his voice, except it sounded like the voice
of a stranger. A demon.

You will not touch her again.

And then, the worst moment of all, the moment that revealed and defined him. The moment Jacob could never
escape or forget.

He raised his clenched fist. His father raised the riding
crop again, preparing to bring another blow onto his daughter. Jacob knew he could not allow that to happen. He would
not. And so he hit his father with all the force and fury of
fifteen years of anger, hurt, disappointment and despair. He
hit him as hard as he could, and in that second of vengeance
he felt a fierce sense of satisfaction, of relief.

And then, worst of all, a sound rent the air. A sound of
wild laughter. Jacob never knew who had laughed—who
could laugh in such a moment. Had his father laughed at the
thought of his son turning against him? Had *he* laughed because it had felt so good—in that one brief second—to finally fight back?

In the dream the sound echoed through him, a raucous,

wild peal. It was the laughter, Jacob always thought, of a madman. Two madmen—for surely they both were, he and his father, in that moment.

'Jacob, *Jacob!*'

The red haze was starting to lift as Jacob heard the voice, high-pitched, familiar, frightened. His eyes jerked open and he awakened as if he'd been doused in ice water. He felt like he had, for his body was drenched in a cold sweat.

Mollie half sat in bed, clutching a sheet to her, her face pale and shocked, her eyes wide and dilated with fear.

Oh, God.

Revulsion swept through Jacob in a humiliating, sickening wave. He knew what Mollie had seen. He knew what she'd heard.

His stomach lurched and in one abrupt movement he rolled out of bed and slammed into the bathroom.

He retched, disgusted with himself more than ever before. From outside he heard a timid knock.

'Jacob...are you...are you all right?'

He rinsed his mouth out and braced his forearms against the sink. His heart was throwing itself against his ribcage as if it had a death wish. Perhaps it did.

He'd never felt so low, so wretched, and that was saying something. That dream defined him. It revealed him, and Mollie had seen him at his worst. His worst...and she was afraid.

'I'm fine,' he said. His voice sounded hoarse. In the mirror his face was pale, his eyes as dilated as Mollie's, his hair dampened and spiky with sweat. Jacob washed his face and resolutely opened the door. He knew how things would have to be now.

He had been a fool ever—even for a single night—to believe in hope.

Mollie stood in the centre of the room, still clutching the

sheet to her chest. Jacob ignored her. He reached into his
suitcase for a fresh T-shirt and shrugged it on, raking his
fingers through his hair, his back to her.

'Jacob…' Her voice sounded so very small.

'What?' He didn't turn around.

'What…? What was…?' She hesitated and then said very
quietly, 'Tell me what happened.'

Jacob shrugged. 'It was just a dream.'

'What kind of dream? You looked as if—' She swallowed.
'Strange.'

Jacob almost laughed again, this time the dry, humourless
laugh of the utterly despairing. He turned around. 'People
sometimes do strange things in dreams, Mollie,' he told her,
his voice sharp with a mocking edge. 'Did I scare you?' He
made it a question of no real interest to him.

'No, of course not,' she said quickly. Too quickly. 'Your
dream scared me,' she clarified. 'It looked like it was…ter-
rible.'

'Really?' He sounded bored now. It was all too easy to
affect these poses, to push her away. He'd had so much practice.

Mollie shook her head, her eyes wide. 'Do you remember
the dream?'

He hesitated, finding it surprisingly hard to lie. Suddenly
it wasn't so easy any more, because even now, when he knew
he couldn't, when he knew how he'd terrified her, he wanted
to tell her everything. He swallowed. 'No.'

Mollie nodded slowly, and Jacob couldn't tell if she believed him or not.

Mollie stared at Jacob, wishing she knew what words to say,
and that she had the strength to say them. His face looked
blank, bored, yet his body was nearly quivering with a tension, an anger, that Mollie couldn't understand.

What had he dreamed about? Why had he been making

that sound—that horrible sound—something halfway between a laugh and a sob? It had been such a terrible, lonely, awful sound; she hadn't even realised it had been coming from Jacob, and when she'd rolled over to look at him she'd seen him in the throes of a terrible dream, a nightmare, the look on his face one of utter agony.

She'd assumed for so long that he was cold, emotionless, even soulless. Now the idea seemed laughable. She'd thought, even that very night, that he'd walked away from his family because he didn't care enough, didn't feel their pain.

Now she knew he felt too much.

'It's late,' Jacob said into the silence of Mollie's own spinning thoughts. 'You should get some sleep.' He walked towards the door.

'Jacob—' Mollie reached one hand out towards him even though his back was to her. She felt the moment slipping away from her, the opportunity to question and comfort and maybe even understand gone—perhaps for ever. 'Aren't you going to come back to bed?' she whispered.

He turned to flash her a grim smile. 'I've had enough sleep for one evening,' he said, and then he walked out of the bedroom, closing the door behind him with a final click.

Mollie stood there for a moment, the sheet still clutched to her naked body. She felt cold and alone and afraid. Too afraid to open that door and ask Jacob to tell her—what? Did she even *want* to know what caused that dream, what memories and regrets lurked inside of him? Could she accept the truth?

Her own cowardice shamed her. Disconsolate, uncertain and suddenly, unbearably sad, Mollie turned back to the bed. Curled up on one side, she had a feeling she wouldn't sleep any more either.

Morning dawned slowly, pale grey fingers of light creeping across the floor of the bedroom. Mollie shifted, every muscle aching. Her eyes were dry and gritty. She must have dozed at least a little bit, but she didn't feel as if she had.

She slid from the bed and tiptoed out of the room, glancing around almost furtively for Jacob. She didn't see him anywhere though, and she retreated to her own bedroom, still filled with a miserable uncertainty. She had no idea what to do now, what would happen next.

A stingingly hot shower helped, as did a fresh change of clothes. Her Italian clothes, a close-fitting cashmere sweater in soft, pussy-willow grey and a pair of skinny designer jeans bolstered her confidence and gave her courage. She pulled her hair back with a scarf and repaired her still-pale face with make-up, then taking a deep breath headed out into the rest of the suite.

Jacob sat at the desk in the living room. He had showered and changed as well, and now wore an immaculate grey suit that made him look gorgeous and very remote. He looked up from his laptop as she entered, and gave her a small, cool smile.

Mollie's heart sank. So that was how it was going to be.

'Would you like some breakfast?' His voice was scrupulously polite, carefully devoid of emotion, just as it had been when she'd first seen him at her cottage. He was a stranger, nothing but a beautiful stranger. He gestured to a table tucked into the corner of the room. 'There are muffins and croissants there, as well as a pot of tea. If you'd prefer something more substantial, I can order it for you.'

Mollie didn't think she could manage a morsel. 'No, thank you,' she said quietly. 'This is enough.'

Jacob turned back to his laptop. 'I'm afraid I can't go to the expo with you today,' he said in that awful, polite voice. 'I have some business to attend to. But I hired a car to take you there.'

'I'm perfectly capable of taking the tube,' Mollie returned stiffly. 'I lived in London for three years.'

Jacob's gaze remained on the screen of his computer. 'If you have the opportunity, why not take it?'

Mollie swallowed down the words *Because I don't want anything from you when you're like this.* She reached for a muffin. 'Are we still returning to Wolfe Manor tonight?'

Jacob glanced up, his body stilling, his eyes so very dark. 'Yes,' he said quietly. 'We'll go back tonight.'

Mollie crumbled the muffin onto the plate. 'Jacob...' He waited, saying nothing, and she made herself go on. 'Why are you being like this? So...remote? Last night—'

'Last night shouldn't have happened,' Jacob cut in, his voice flat. Mollie felt the blood drain from her face. She should have expected this, based on his attitude this morning, yet it still hurt, like blood drawn straight from her heart.

'Why not?' she whispered.

Surprise flashed briefly across Jacob's features, as if he hadn't expected her to ask that question. She wondered if he would answer it honestly, or at all. 'Mollie...' He began, his voice low, and she knew this was all the opening she would ever get.

'Jacob, what happened last night was real. I know it was. This—' she flung an arm out as if to encompass the tension tautening the very air between them '—this isn't. This is *fake.*'

'You don't know what's real,' he said quietly.

'The dream wasn't,' Mollie told him. She could feel her heart pounding so hard it hurt. She spoke from a deep instinct that the dream had changed everything. Ruined it. And right now she was damned if she would let it. 'That dream wasn't real, Jacob. It was just a dream. A nightmare. Why won't you trust me?'

He didn't answer, just stared at her with that infuriatingly blank expression. What seethed beneath the surface? Why wouldn't he tell her?

'Jacob, what do you dream about? What haunts you so, even now? Was it something that happened in your childhood? Is that why you ran away?' She felt as if she were stumbling through the dark, her hands stretched out in front of her like a child's. 'Is it your father? Or Annabelle—'

'So many options,' he drawled. Mollie recoiled from that light, scornful tone. 'I had such an *unhappy* childhood. A therapist would have a field day.'

'I'm not your therapist—'

'You sound like you're trying to be.'

'No,' Mollie retorted, her voice rising in frustration. 'I'm trying to tell you that we can work through this...together—'

'Stop it, Mollie.' He snapped his laptop shut, rising from the desk in one graceful movement. His back was to her. 'Forget the dream. Forget it all.'

'I can't.' Her throat felt as if it were closing in on itself, as if she could barely speak. 'Can you?' she managed. She saw his shoulders stiffen, his body tense. She waited, afraid to say any more, afraid she might beg. Cry.

'I have to,' Jacob said. His voice sounded quiet and even sad. She saw his head bow, his shoulders slump for an instant before he straightened again to his normal militarily precise posture...just as he'd been doing his whole life. Being strong. Taking all the weight. All the guilt.

'No, you don't,' Mollie said. 'You don't.'

He shook his head, his back still to her. 'There are things you don't understand.'

'Stop using that as your excuse and *tell* me.'

He shook his head again, and she thought she heard him make a choked sound, almost like a cry. Yet when he finally turned around, she wished he hadn't. He looked so resigned, so resolute, so *sad*. 'I don't want to tell you. If I do, it will change how you think of me, and I couldn't bear that.'

Her heart twisted, tore. A tear trembled on her eyelash and then slipped silently down her cheek. 'And you're not willing even to risk it? For...for us?'

'There is no us.'

'There could be.' She *was* begging. And crying.

'No, Mollie.' Now Jacob sounded regretful, and very, very final. 'I'm sorry, but there isn't and there will never be. There can't be.' He paused, drawing a shuddering breath. 'Sometimes I wish there could. I wish I was different but I know myself and I know what I'm capable of—what I have inside of me. And it's not enough for a woman like you.'

'What is that supposed to mean?' Mollie asked. She heard the brokenness of her own voice; she couldn't even hide her heartache.

'It means that you are a warm and wonderful and loving person, and you deserve and need someone far better than me.'

'That sounds like an excuse.'

'I wish it was. That would be easier.' He rubbed a hand across his face, looking so tired and lonely and lost that Mollie wanted to put her arms around him and draw him to her. As if sensing that need in her, Jacob looked up sharply. 'You can't save people, Mollie. Just like you said. You were right.'

'I know you can't save people, Jacob. I told you that yesterday. I don't want to *save* you—'

'You do. You might not think you do, but I can see it in your eyes. You think you can help me. Heal me. But you can't. And trust me, I'm not worth saving anyway.'

Mollie let out a sound that trembled between a laugh and a sob. 'Yes, you are.'

He shook his head. 'If you knew—but it doesn't matter. *I* know. And I know there can be no future for us. I'm sorry to have taken advantage of you last night. I thought I could control myself, but I—I couldn't.' His voice trembled for an instant. 'I failed. I failed you….'

Rage tore through her heart, spilled into her words. 'Last night was *not* a failure. Last night was a success, one of the most beautiful things that has ever—'

'It was,' Jacob agreed quietly. He smiled, sadly, and

Mollie felt her heart break. It was a physical thing, as if her body were being cut in half. She could hardly breathe for the pain of it, and she understood why they called it a break. It wasn't an ache, or a soreness, or a twinging pain; it was too agonising for that. Too final. Jacob crossed the room and reached out to wipe the tear still trickling down her cheek. 'It *was* beautiful,' he said, and still smiling that achingly sorrowful smile, he turned away. 'I'll have my driver get the car for you,' he said, and then he was gone.

CHAPTER EIGHT

MOLLIE walked through the expo practically on tiptoes, as if she were made of glass. Bubbles, and they were popping slowly, one by one, so that when they were all gone there would be nothing left.

She barely took in the sights that only yesterday had fired her imagination. Everything seemed to hold a memory; she could hardly walk through the hall without picturing Jacob by her side, listening to her wild ramble of ideas, offering his little suggestions, smiling faintly.

How could it hurt so much, after so little time?

She felt only relief when the day came to a close, even though it meant she'd see Jacob again, which she both desired and dreaded.

In fact, she didn't see him until he lightly touched her shoulder. She'd been standing in front of the Zen garden exhibit again, recalling his words from yesterday: *I have no trouble believing the world possesses imperfections. Or that they exist in myself. But to embrace them...*

She understood what he meant now. Not only could Jacob not accept the imperfections in himself, he couldn't forgive them. Forgive himself.

What could he not forgive? Mollie wondered helplessly. Was it the night he hit his father? Surely he knew that was self-defence. Or was there something else—something she was afraid to know? *Would* it change everything, like Jacob had said?

'Did you have a good day?' Jacob asked, his hand resting lightly on her shoulder for only a second, and startled, Mollie turned around.

A good day? Was he *joking*? 'Not really,' she said rather flatly, and Jacob simply nodded in acceptance.

'The car's outside.'

No more red sports car, Mollie soon saw. This was not a joyful jaunt in the countryside with the top down. Instead Jacob had hired a limo with acres of space between them and a driver at the wheel.

She slid into the leather luxury with a sharp little smile. 'What happened to the convertible?'

He shrugged. 'I'm leaving it in the city for a bit. I'm afraid I have to work on the way back.' He didn't sound remotely apologetic as he snapped open his briefcase and took out a sheaf of papers. Mollie turned to stare out the window. It was a good thing they hadn't taken the convertible, she thought drearily. It had started to rain.

As the limo turned off the motorway and Mollie saw the sign for Wolfestone with a little tremor of dread, she finally summoned the courage to break the silence.

'So what now?'

Jacob stilled. He looked up, his expression composed, although Mollie saw a flicker of wariness in his dark eyes. She was good at reading him now, at even understanding him. Even though she still didn't understand—or know—enough.

'What now?' he repeated carefully. 'I imagine you have a bit more work to complete on the gardens.'

'Another fortnight and it will be finished. I'll be finished,' she emphasised starkly. Jacob said nothing and she made herself ask, 'So we just go on for the next two weeks as if nothing has happened?'

As if you didn't come in and shatter my world?

'Perhaps it would be better if we didn't see each other,' Jacob said after a moment. 'A clean break.'

Mollie shook her head slowly. 'You really have some nerve, you know that?'

'I know you're hurt, Mollie—'

'Do you?' She thrust her face towards him, her eyes sparkling with both tears and rage. 'Do you *know* that, Jacob? Empirically? Intellectually? What about with your heart?'

'I told you—'

'Oh, I *know*.' Mollie slapped her hand to her forehead. 'That's one thing I know, right? Because you told me. But all the things you *won't* tell me—about the man you supposedly really are—I'm just supposed to take that on trust. Right?' She didn't wait for him to answer. 'How very convenient for you,' Mollie told him. 'You can just walk away when it gets too much because you're so *sorry* but you can't help it. You've got all these terrible secrets, but you won't even tell me what they are! You know what that makes you, Jacob?' She glared at him, trembling with anger and hurt, but Jacob's expression didn't even flicker.

'What does it make me?' he asked quietly.

'A coward,' Mollie spat. Vindication didn't feel nearly as good as she wanted it to. 'It makes you a coward.'

Jacob accepted her scorn without comment. He nodded his acceptance as the limo pulled up to Wolfe Manor. It was raining heavily now, a steady, drumming downpour. Mollie stared at him, wanting *something*, but he didn't speak. He didn't even change expression. And with a choked sob, she wrenched open the car door, grabbing her case from the driver, and headed off into the rain.

Jacob watched the rain and fog swallow Mollie as she stormed away from him, disappearing through the hedges that were no more than dark shapes in the sudden storm. He closed his eyes for a second and steeled his soul.

Calm. Control.

Coward.

He deserved her scorn, he knew. He accepted it as his due. How could he accept anything else, when she had no idea why he'd walk away from the best thing in his life? No clue as to just what kind of man he was?

The kind of man who could hit his father in cold, cold blood. Who raised his hand to his own sister. Who walked away.

Jacob slammed out of the limo. He didn't need thoughts like this. He didn't need to lash himself with the whip of regret. He'd felt its unrelenting sting too many times already. He'd moved forward in his life, and part of that was accepting what was and was not possible. What he could and could not have.

He'd made peace with it long ago, or at least he thought he had.

Then he'd returned to Wolfe Manor, to his old life, and all the old ghosts and memories rose up to taunt him with what he could never have. Who he could never be. And in the middle of it all, Mollie. Making him wonder and wish and want in a way he never had before.

Striding into the manor, Jacob shrugged off his suit jacket and dropped his briefcase by the door. All around him the manor echoed emptily, silently, yet he still heard the whispers. Felt them.

His gaze, as it so often did, travelled to the sweeping staircase, rested at its foot where his sister had huddled in a helpless, foetal ball while his father whipped the very life out of her. Standing there, Jacob could almost see her, hear his brothers' desperate cries as they tugged on their father to stop his brutal abuse.

Stop it, Dad. Please, stop it...

And he felt—as he so often did these days—the answering rage in himself when he'd seen that pathetic, terrible scene; it was a rage that flowed like fire through his veins and made his pulse hammer and his fists clench. He felt it, even now, twenty years later, and it was an anger so consuming it nearly frightened him.

This he did not know how to control.

This was why he would never let someone like Mollie into his life, someone who could be hurt, or even destroyed by what he was.

Someone he could love.

Mollie threw herself into her work with the energy and drive of the obsessed. She woke as dawn was spreading its pearly fingers across the sky, pulled on her boots and her work clothes and headed out into the gardens when they were still fresh with dew. She worked all day, weeding and pruning and planting, only stopping to drink some water and eat an apple or a quick sandwich. She returned to the cottage at night, when darkness finally made it impossible to continue, and fell into bed sweaty and exhausted, yet still with enough energy to think. Remember. And wish things—*Jacob*—could be different.

As the days passed she told herself that it was better this way, for both her and Jacob. She asked herself if they could have ever really had a relationship, and made herself answer no.

The reasons were obvious and unrelenting. Other than these few short weeks on the Wolfe estate, they had separate lives. Separate dreams. Separate everything.

And Jacob had too many dark secrets, deep regrets. Mollie knew she could never understand or come to love until she knew those…and Jacob clearly had no intention of letting that happen.

And what did love have to do with it anyway? she asked herself as she headed back to the cottage one afternoon to change into more decent clothes. She was meeting the tree surgeon at two o'clock and knew she should look at least somewhat presentable. She hurried upstairs, distracted by her own racing thoughts.

Love had nothing to do with it. She didn't even know Jacob well enough to love him, or wonder if she could love him. They'd spent a handful of days together, days out of time, out of reality. It was ridiculous to think it could amount to anything. It was absurd to still feel so bereft.

Yet she did. Memories played through her mind like music, haunting, discordant notes that created a symphony of longing. She saw Jacob's small smile, that little tug on the corner of his mouth that reached right down inside of her. She remembered how he'd thought to show her her father's rose, and how he'd given her the gift of boots after the rip in her own had ruined his rug. And then the more painful memories of lips and hands and skin, of feeling complete and whole and *known* in his arms, and wanting it again, wanting it for ever.

Groaning aloud, Mollie changed quickly and dragged a brush through her unruly curls.

'Stop it, stop it, stop it,' she muttered, and hurried towards the narrow, twisting staircase she'd gone up and down a thousand times. Her foot caught on the broken brass runner at the top of the stair and in slow motion, so she almost felt as if she were witnessing the whole excruciating episode from a distance; she fell down those steep, narrow stairs, head over heels, feeling each jarring bump in every bone in her body, before she landed at the bottom, smacking her temple hard against the stone hearth of the fireplace.

She heard the resounding thwack; it was the last thing she heard. Before she could even register a thought besides *That hurt*, her world went black.

Jacob had been feeling out of sorts ever since he had returned from London and left Mollie storming off in the rain.

He hadn't seen her since. He'd glimpsed her from a distance, working in the garden, and he'd wanted to go out there and snatch her into his arms, kiss away his reservations and regrets, forget the past and its awful secrets, or at least pretend they didn't matter.

He didn't.

He couldn't.

Instead he immersed himself in work, overseeing the design of a new eco-friendly office building in Rio de Janeiro. He checked on the work on Wolfe Manor, telling himself he was relieved to see that it was progressing nicely. He could put the place on the market by the end of the month.

Why did that thought now make him ache in a way he never had before? He'd never had an affection for this place, never wanted to darken its door again. Yet the thought of leaving it, leaving all the memories behind as if they'd never been, suddenly seemed both unwanted and impossible.

How can you start fresh, without first dealing with the past?

He'd asked that question of Mollie. He'd convinced her she needed to stay and make the garden whole, that it would be a way of redeeming those lost, lonely years with her father.

Redemption was possible for her.

He'd never thought it was for him. He couldn't start fresh; he couldn't deal with the past.

You've got all these terrible secrets, but you won't even tell me what they are....

The only way he could deal with the past was to speak of it. Admit the truth to Mollie. Even if he lost her, at least he would have been honest.

You know what that makes you, Jacob? A coward.

Yes, Jacob thought, Mollie was right. He *was* a coward. He'd told Mollie she didn't know or understand him, and he knew why.

Because you never gave her a chance.

The sound of someone knocking at the front door of the manor jolted him out of his thoughts, and he strode to it, feeling relief at the interruption.

'Mr...' The man on the doorstep looked down at his work order dubiously. 'Wolfe?'

'Yes?'

'I was supposed to meet your landscaper at two o'clock at the garden gate. Nobody showed up and she hasn't answered her mobile so I wondered if you knew what was going on?' His voice lilted upwards hopefully, and Jacob frowned as he checked his watch. It was half past two. If Mollie had made an appointment, he knew she'd keep it. She'd been working feverishly these past few days. He'd seen her in the garden as dawn lit the sky and as dusk settled.

'She's not here,' he told the tree surgeon tersely. 'She's probably in the gardens somewhere, and she lost track of time.' Yet he realised he was speaking as much to himself as to the man in front of him, and he heard the thread of fear in his voice, felt it snake coldly through his body. 'I'll go have a look,' he said, and the man followed him around the house to the gardens.

By silent, mutual agreement, they separated, moving in different directions to cover more of the extensive grounds. Jacob strode through the terraced gardens, their neat rows open and exposed, seeing quickly that Mollie wasn't there. He went to the Children's Garden, remembering how she'd sat musing under the lilac bush, her smooth forehead puckered into a frown, the way she'd smiled when she'd seen him. She wasn't there. The Rose Garden was completely empty, the beds still neatly ploughed under.

Where was she?

Finally he headed to the place he probably should have checked first: the cottage. It sat in its hidden little garden, dark and still. He knocked on the front door, but the sound just echoed.

After a second's pause Jacob turned the handle and poked his head around the door. 'Mollie…?' he called, and then he saw her.

Jacob cursed viciously as he flung the door wide and hurried over to where Mollie lay sprawled at the bottom of stairs, blood trickling down her cheek. For a moment he felt a terrible sense of déjà vu; it roiled through him in a sickening wave and he nearly stumbled.

Again. It had happened again. And once again he'd been too late.

He bent, turning her over, feeling how light and fragile she seemed in his arms. Her head lolled back and he saw the vivid purple bruise on her forehead.

She'd fallen, he realised. She'd fallen on the damn stairs. He scooped her up, cradling her against his body as he reached for his mobile, and with his free hand stabbed the numbers 999.

Mollie came slowly to consciousness, like a swimmer rising to the surface of the water. She felt heavy, as if her limbs were weighted down. And her head throbbed abominably.

Her eyes fluttered open and she blinked at the bright light. She was in a hospital room, sterile and neat, a view of sky and trees visible from the one window. And Jacob stood next to it, his back to her, staring out at the darkening sky.

She must have made some small sound, for he turned suddenly, gazing at her with an intense anxiety that had emotion clogging her throat and stinging her eyes. She tried to smile.

'How bad do I look?'

'Pretty bad.' Jacob gave her a small smile, although Mollie could see his eyes were still dark and shadowed. 'And wonderful. I was worried about you. You've been unconscious for six hours.'

'Goodness.' Mollie closed her eyes again as the world swam sickeningly. 'How stupid of me.'

'Do you know what happened?'

'I think I fell down the stairs.' She winced. 'Rather hard.'

'If you hadn't had that appointment with the tree surgeon...' Jacob said, breaking off suddenly. Mollie opened her eyes and saw his face tense, twist.

'What...?' she whispered.

'You could have lain there for hours,' Jacob said savagely. 'And nobody would have known. You could have died.'

She tried to smile, but even that hurt. 'I would have woken up and crawled to the phone.'

'I'm serious, Mollie. I've been staying away from you for both of our sakes and look what happened.'

'Tell me you're not going to blame yourself for this too,' Mollie said. 'Please.' Jacob felt silent, and she shook her head. 'Jacob, you cannot take the whole bloody world on your shoulders. You're not God. You're not even Atlas.' His mouth tightened, his eyes flashing, but she continued anyway. 'I fell down the stairs. It was an *accident*.' She thought of Annabelle, and how her father had whipped her at the bottom of the manor stairs. She knew that much. 'It's not like before, Jacob,' she whispered. 'It's not your fault.'

'If I—'

'No ifs.' She cut him off, even though it made her head throb. 'What were you going to do? Check up on me every half-hour? Tuck me into bed?' That made her think of other things, other memories, so she hurried on. 'I'm an adult. Accidents happen. I'm just glad the tree surgeon had the foresight to seek you out when I didn't show up.' She smiled at him, wanting to smooth the deep crease between his eyebrows. 'And that you had the tenacity to look for me—and find me.'

Jacob met her gaze, saw her smile. Mollie felt the tug between them; it was still there. It had always been there, perhaps even when she'd been a child. Even then she'd been drawn to him, to his tall, dark presence, to the strength and stability of him. 'Even so,' Jacob said, his words final, 'it won't happen again.'

Mollie leaned her head back against the pillow. 'Well, I'll try not to trip. I need to fix the runner.'

'No,' Jacob replied. 'You're not going back to the cottage. You'll stay at Wolfe Manor with me.'

CHAPTER NINE

'What?' Mollie struggled up to a sitting position, only to fall back against the pillows, exhausted. 'That's not necessary—'

'Yes, it is.'

'For you, maybe, and your overblown sense of duty,' she snapped. She was tired of Jacob's staggering sense of responsibility for everyone and everything. She couldn't compete with it. 'I'm perfectly fine without you.' That wasn't completely true, but she could certainly live alone like any normal adult.

'That may be, but I'm not risking something like this happening again.'

'Why don't you just put a monitor on me?' Mollie demanded waspishly. 'Or imbed a computer chip in my head?'

Jacob smiled faintly, although his eyes were hard with determination. 'That's not a bad idea.'

Mollie let out a short, dry laugh and closed her eyes. She took a deep breath. 'Jacob,' she said, opening them, 'you are not responsible for me.'

'You're my employee,' Jacob replied calmly, 'so, in point of fact, I am.'

'Not like that.' He said nothing and Mollie knew there was something bigger going on here, something that stretched back into the years, its roots going deep into the spoiled soil of the Wolfe family. 'It's not your fault I fell down the stairs,' she said clearly. 'It's not your fault your father hit your sister, or did any of the terrible things he did.' She paused, for Jacob had gone utterly still, his expression seeming to close in on itself, blank and fathomless. 'It's not your fault,' Mollie continued quietly, 'that things fell apart when you left. You need to—'

'You're going to tell me what I need?' Jacob cut in. His voice was polite yet very cold. Now Mollie was the one to still.

'I just—'

'But you blamed me as much as anyone else, Mollie,' Jacob told her softly. 'It's my fault your father didn't have a job for so many years. It's my fault the two of you were struggling alone for so long, forgotten, invisible. Hell, maybe it's my fault that he suffered from dementia. Maybe it wouldn't have happened if I'd stayed, if the manor had been something he could hold onto.' Mollie stared at him, what little colour she had draining from her face, too shocked to utter a word. 'So,' Jacob continued in that same soft, lethal voice, 'why should I believe you now? If you thought all that was my fault, how do you think my brothers and sister felt?'

From somewhere Mollie found her voice, hoarse and scratchy. 'They've forgiven you, Jacob. I know Annabelle has….'

'I know they have,' Jacob told her. He sounded scornful. 'I've seen every one of them since I've been back. I've faced their anger and their confusion and their hurt. And I've asked for their forgiveness.' He paused, his breath coming fast now. 'Do you think that makes any *difference*?'

Mollie could only stare. His words were hammer blows to her heart, for she knew he'd spoken the truth. She *had* blamed him. They all had. Jacob had shouldered all the guilt and all the responsibility, and they'd let him, they'd given it to him, even though she—and undoubtedly all his siblings— had said they hadn't.

'I'm sorry,' she finally whispered, and shrugging a shoulder, Jacob turned away.

'It doesn't matter,' he said, his back to her, his voice low. 'It's not just about what you see as my overblown sense of responsibility.' He drew a breath. 'I blame myself, Mollie, because of who I am and what I did…not what I *didn't* do.' He turned to face her, his eyes bleak. 'There's no escaping or forgiving that.'

Mollie stared at him, speechless, unable to think of any comforting words. She felt as if Jacob had retreated farther from her than ever before…and she couldn't help but wonder if this time it was her fault.

The next day the hospital released her. Jacob drove her back to Wolfe Manor. When he pulled up in front of the big house, Mollie made no objection. She followed him into the house's dim, cool foyer, knowing that after all that had been said—all she'd realised—she wasn't going to stand on her self-righteous pride and indignation now.

'I chose one of the newly renovated bedrooms for you,' Jacob told her. 'I hope it's suitable.' He spoke in that awful, distant voice that made Mollie want to cry. It made it hard to believe that he'd ever kissed her tears or held her in his arms, or that they'd made love.

'I'm sure it's fine.'

'The doctor told you to take it easy for at least a few more days,' Jacob continued. 'I hope you will abide by that. I've made arrangements for some day labourers to come in and do the heavy work in the garden.'

'That's fine. I can give instructions from here. It's just a matter of doing the manual work, except for the Rose Garden.'

'The Rose Garden?'

'I haven't settled on a design,' Mollie admitted. Every time she thought of it, the whole idea defeated her. The Rose

Garden had been her father's idea of landscaping perfection. How could she change it, much less design something of her own? 'I think I'll go rest now,' she said, because she couldn't stand to be near Jacob when he was like this, cold and formal and so very distant.

'I had your things removed from the cottage. They're in your bedroom.'

Mollie nodded and turned away. She felt Jacob watching her all the way up the stairs.

The next few days fell into a disheartening pattern of impersonal solicitude. Jacob excused himself to the study most of the time, and Mollie didn't bother ever going in there or even knocking on the door. She hated that room, and she had a feeling Jacob did as well.

She worked on designs for the Rose Garden, although every sketch she began she ended up tossing in frustration. All her plans just seemed like a shallow version of what had already been there.

Yet the rest of the garden was nearly finished. From the window she saw the new paving stones, the weeded flower beds, the pruned trees. The grass on the terraced lawns glittered like emerald velvet. The house, too, was emerging from its chrysalis of dust cloths and scaffolding; the downstairs was completely finished, the paint fresh, the window coverings and carpets restored or replaced as needed. It was beautiful, if impersonal, and Mollie wondered who would buy the house when Jacob actually put it on the market. Who would live there, love it? Even with its new patina of fresh paint, the house still seethed with unhappy memories...or so it felt to Mollie, as she wandered its empty rooms.

Upstairs the bedrooms had been renovated as well; the photographs on Annabelle's walls had been removed, and Mollie wondered what Jacob had done with them. Perhaps a decorator had thrown them out. Perhaps Jacob hadn't cared about them at all.

Mollie knew she was being contrary. A few weeks ago she'd been annoyed and embarrassed that Jacob had seen all those revealing candids of her. Now she wanted him to be a hiding a snap under his pillow? She was ridiculous.

One rainy afternoon when even the labourers had to leave the garden work, Mollie wandered upstairs to the third floor of the manor. From the peeling wallpaper, a faded pattern of blowsy cabbage roses, to the cobweb spangling every corner, it appeared this floor had not yet been renovated or even touched. Mollie wondered if it had been completely forgotten.

Curious and a little wary, she made her way up the narrow stairs, and pushed open the door at the end of the hallway.

Pale, watery sunlight, breaking through the rain clouds of earlier, streamed through the long, narrow windows, revealing a thick layer of dust on the old wooden floorboards. They creaked as Mollie carefully moved across the room, taking it all in.

It was a nursery. It looked like something out of a Victorian novel with a moth-eaten rocking horse in one corner, an elaborate wooden dollhouse in another. Rusted tin soldiers lined up on one windowsill, ready to march.

There were some newer toys too—some building bricks, a few tatty board games, signs that the Wolfe children had once lived and played here. The air was thick with the dust Mollie had stirred up simply by walking across the floor, so with some effort she opened the windows and breathed in the rain-damp air. Then she turned back to the room.

A few childish drawings and scribbles had been taped to the wall, and she moved closer to inspect them. A princess drawing by Annabelle, an elaborate map of the estate, laboriously inked in intricate detail, with two childish signatures in the bottom corner: *Jacob and Lucas Wolfe, ages 9 and 8.*

On a rickety table in one corner there was a model of the house, built, she saw, from lolly sticks and toothpicks. She smiled faintly, thinking of how Jacob must have cherished architectural dreams even at a young age. She imagined him here, concentrating on his precious model, the other children looking on in interest. Perhaps this house did hold some happy memories.

Another paper taped to the wall had an important-looking list of everyone's birthday, as well as what kind of cake they preferred and what presents they wanted. Mollie's gaze ran down the list, stopping in surprise when she saw Jacob's birthday was, in fact, tomorrow. And when he'd been eight years old he'd wanted a double chocolate cake and a chess set.

'What are you doing here?'

Mollie whirled around, stirring up more dust. Jacob stood in the doorway, and from the tone of his voice and the expression on his face Mollie didn't think he was very glad to see her here.

'Sorry…I was just poking around. I don't think this place has been touched in twenty years.'

'More like thirty. I saw the door to the stairs was open and wondered if the renovators had finally made their way up here.' Jacob glanced around the room with a dispassionate air. 'It's filthy. I'll have to get them to clear it all out. Everything else is just about finished.'

'Oh, don't,' Mollie said impulsively. 'There are so many memories here—'

'I know.' The two words were clipped.

'Good ones though,' she persisted. 'At least, they feel that way to me. Look—did you make this?' She pulled on his arm, surprising them both by her touch, and after a second's pause Jacob reluctantly let her lead him to the corner of the room. He glanced at the model of the house without any expression at all.

'Yes, I made it.'

'It's amazing! You showed your talent even then.' He shrugged, but Mollie persisted, feeling some deep-seated need to show Jacob all these treasures, to help him reclaim the good parts of his past. 'Look at this…you and Lucas drew this map?'

Now he smiled faintly. 'Yes…I'd forgotten about that. We spent ages on it. We were measuring the lawns with a slide rule, trying to make sure we got it exactly to scale. One inch for every one hundred yards, if I remember correctly.'

'It's incredibly complex, considering how young you were.' She glanced around again at the dusty room. 'Did you spend much time here?'

'No, not really. Holidays mostly. Lucas and I went to boarding school when we were quite young.' He paused, and Mollie held her breath, knowing he was going to tell her more. Perhaps he even wanted to. 'My father never came looking for us up here,' Jacob said softly. 'Sometimes it felt like the only place we were really safe.'

Mollie blinked, swallowed the sudden thickening of tears in her throat. Silently, because there were no words, she reached for his hand. To her surprise and joy, Jacob let her fingers slide through his, and held on.

After a moment he nodded towards the old dollhouse. 'Annabelle could play with that for hours. She used to rope me into playing with her. I was always the father.' He smiled wryly, his eyes now alight with memories. 'And Nathaniel loved the dress-up box.' He gestured to a chest in the corner; Mollie saw the dull gleam of a knight's helmet and toy sword. 'We used to have mock battles.' Lost as he was in a rare moment of nostalgia, Mollie knew he didn't hear the thread of love in his voice, or realize how he'd made sure all of his siblings had memories they could cherish…memories he'd made happen.

He turned slowly around in the room, taking it all in,

the sunlight breaking through the clouds and washing over him, his features softened with remembrance. And in that moment Mollie knew she loved him.

It seemed so amazingly apparent, so utterly obvious. So *simple*. As the realisation rippled through her body, her heart's answering response was, *Of course.*

Of course she loved him. She'd started to love him even when she was a child, peeking between the hedges. She loved the boy he'd been, trying to take care of his family, and the man he'd become, responsible, gentle, utterly trustworthy.

Her mind had tried to convince her she didn't love him, that she didn't even know him well enough to love him, but in that moment Mollie knew she did. Perhaps she always had.

Yet she knew she couldn't tell him now. Her heart was filled to overflowing, yet Mollie swallowed it back down. It would be too much for Jacob now. So she just smiled and touched his arm. 'How wonderful,' she said, 'that you all had one another.'

Jacob looked at her, blinking as if he was surprised by the realisation. 'Yes,' he said slowly, 'it was.'

With the realisation that she loved Jacob, everything else seemed to slide into place. It was as if her love for him was the key that unlocked not just her heart, but her mind. Her ideas. Now she knew just what to do with the Rose Garden.

Yet first there was something more important to attend to: Jacob's birthday. Since he'd closeted himself in the office for most of the day, preparing was easy. She left him a note in the kitchen letting him know she'd gone into town, and walked the quarter mile to the bus stop in the centre of Wolfestone. Her shopping took less than an hour, and when she returned to the manor she saw that Jacob had not seen her note or even left his study at all.

Just as well, Mollie decided with a new, optimistic determination. This would give her more time to make things just as she wanted them.

That evening she changed into a strappy top and a summery skirt that swung about her legs, tamed her hair and touched up her make-up. Then she went to Jacob's study and rapped sharply on the door.

'Mollie...?' His voice, from behind the thick oak, was muffled.

'It's eight o'clock, Jacob. Aren't you going to stop working?'

'I'm sorry. I have a great many things to do.'

Mollie sighed. She'd anticipated this. 'It's just that I'm feeling a little woozy all of a sudden...' She let her voice trail off, and within seconds Jacob had thrown open the door, his face harsh with concern.

'What happened? Are you—?'

'I'm fine.' Mollie grinned at him. 'That was the only way I could think of getting you out of there.'

Jacob stared, completely thunderstruck. 'You lied to me?'

'It was for a noble purpose.' She tugged on his arm before he could work up any real indignation. The man's moral code was unfaltering. 'Come on.'

'What...? I have to—'

'You don't have to do anything right now,' Mollie said. 'Except follow me.' She led him into the kitchen, where she'd dimmed the lights. 'Close your eyes.'

'What...?'

Laughing, Mollie stood on her tiptoes and reached up to cover Jacob's eyes with her hands. 'I mean it.'

Jacob let out a short, irritated breath, and Mollie knew he had no idea what she was doing, or why.

She led him into the centre of the kitchen, her hand still covering his eyes. 'Now, I have to let go for a minute, but no peeking, all right?'

'Right.' He still sounded annoyed.

Mollie dashed over to the light the candles on the cake—all thirty-eight of them. She picked up the cake and brought it front of Jacob; his eyes were still closed.

'All right, you can open them now.'

Jacob's eyes flew open, and Mollie smiled. 'Happy birthday, Jacob.'

He stared at the cake as if he didn't know what it was. He looked so nonplussed Mollie was afraid she'd made a terrible mistake. 'Haven't you ever seen a birthday cake before?' she teased.

His eyes met hers and he gave her a rueful smile. 'Not one for me.'

Mollie stared at him, too surprised to dissemble. 'Not ever?'

He shrugged. 'Not that I remember. My birthday always fell at term time, and the school didn't run to making cakes.'

'Well, I made your favourite,' she said with a smile. 'Double chocolate. At least, that's what you wanted for your eighth birthday. I don't know about now.'

'I love chocolate,' Jacob said, and his voice sounded almost hoarse. Mollie felt the tension spin out between them, tautening and stretching, and her hands nearly trembled as she held the cake.

'Here.' She placed it on the worktop. 'Make a wish.'

Jacob's gaze remained fastened on hers as he bent down to blow out the candles. Mollie held her breath. She certainly knew what she would wish for.

'What did you wish for?' Mollie asked after he'd blown them out. She sounded breathless.

'Now if I told you, it wouldn't come true.' A smile, slow and sexy, curled Jacob's mouth. Mollie felt heat flood through her body. She'd never seen him smile like that before. It made him look unbearably desirable, so that she could barely hold the knife steady as she turned to the cake.

'Let me cut you a piece.' She cut a generous slice and put it on a plate, yet his smile still warmed right through her and gave her the courage to take a forkful and hold it aloft, offering him her own wicked smile. 'Ready?'

Jacob's gaze, dark and hot, never left hers as he obediently opened his mouth. Mollie fed him the cake, her heart starting an uneven, heavy rhythm at the sheer sensuality of the action. She loved him so much. She wanted him so much.

His lips closed around the fork, his hand brushing her fingers. She nearly shuddered aloud. He ate, swallowed and then took the fork from her. 'Now your turn.'

'Wh...what?' Smiling, Jacob reached for the cake. Mollie watched, mesmerised, as he discarded the fork and took a piece, sticky with chocolate, in his fingers and held it aloft. 'You like chocolate, don't you?'

'Oh...yes.' She opened her mouth obediently, like a little bird. Jacob fed her the cake, his thumb brushing her lip; and as she ate, her tongue touched his thumb and made her whole body quiver with desperate awareness. Somehow she managed to swallow, speak. *'Jacob...'*

He pulled her towards him, easily, for she offered no resistance. Her head fell back as his lips brushed hers so briefly, so barely, and Mollie waited, hoping that he would deepen the kiss.

He didn't.

His lips hovered over hers for a torturous second before he stepped back. 'A birthday present,' he said, trying to smile. 'For me.' Even though his voice remained light Mollie saw the struggle in his eyes. She knew he wanted to kiss her again, and more deeply, and even more than that. And yet he wouldn't, whether it was because of responsibility or fear or guilt Mollie couldn't even guess. She wanted to shake him. She wanted to tell him that she might be the best thing that ever happened to him, if only he'd let her love him.

Yet she swallowed the words, because she knew Jacob

wasn't ready to hear them. She wasn't sure she was ready to say them. She certainly was not prepared for the possible—maybe even probable—rejection.

So she smiled, as if that kiss hadn't stripped away her defences and left her shaken and exposed before him, and reached for the box she'd left on the table. 'Actually, I have another present for you.'

'You do?'

'Don't sound so surprised. It is your birthday after all.'

'It's just...no one's ever given me a present before. On my birthday.'

Mollie frowned, the box still in her hands. 'Nobody? What about your brothers and sister? What about the list up in the nursery?'

'List?'

'On the wall. It's how I knew you liked chocolate. It was a list of everyone's birthdays and what they wanted for a present.'

'Oh.' Jacob's expression cleared and he smiled in memory. 'I wrote that list. To keep track, so I wouldn't forget anyone's birthday.'

'Oh, I see.' And she did. How she loved this man. Mollie swallowed past the lump in her throat. She didn't need to ask who remembered Jacob's birthday. The answer was obvious. 'Well, here's your first present.' She handed him the box. Jacob took it, turned it over in his hands. Mollie gave a little laugh. 'You're meant to open it, you know.'

'Yes.' He smiled ruefully, his eyes glinting. 'I suppose I'm just savouring the moment.' Almost reluctantly he slid off the ribbon and tore the wrapping paper.

He gazed down at it for a long moment until Mollie felt compelled to say, 'It's...it's a chess set. On that list you wrote—'

'Yes,' Jacob said quietly. 'I remember.'

He was still staring down at the set Mollie had bought in

town. There hadn't been too many options, and suddenly she wished she'd bought something else, something better, or at least a better chess set, one with marble pieces or a fancy board. She'd bought him a *toy*, for heaven's sake, and he was a millionaire. He could buy a thousand chess sets if he wanted, or one made of solid gold.

Jacob looked up, his eyes bright. 'Thank you,' he said quietly, and Mollie heard the raw note of sincerity in his voice. 'Thank you, Mollie.'

And then she knew she'd bought him the right gift. 'You're welcome.'

They remained there a moment, hesitating, awkward, and Mollie wanted to close the space between them and wrap her arms around Jacob, smooth the furrow from his forehead, kiss his faint smile into fullness. Yet she didn't, because she could see even now Jacob was trying to distance himself, struggling with the gratitude and joy he felt and the guilt and shame that seemed constantly poised to overwhelm him.

Yet she had to touch him, if only a little bit, so leaning forward, she placed a hand on his cheek. Jacob started at the touch, and his eyes closed briefly before he snapped them open, stared at her with those fathomlessly dark eyes so she had no idea what he was thinking. 'Good night, Jacob,' she whispered, and she left the room before he could.

It was too much. He *felt* too much. After years, decades, of nurturing that numbing control, it was finally starting to splinter. And Jacob didn't know what to do without it. How to act. How to be. What to feel.

He let out a long, shuddering sigh as he heard Mollie climb the front stairs. He imagined he could still feel the warmth of her hand on his cheek, and every impulse urged him to follow her up the stairs, to take her in his arms, to stay there for ever.

This was no longer about seduction or sex. He wasn't

dealing with the seemingly simplistic matters of a physical transaction, or resisting it.

No, now something far greater was at stake. It played havoc with his mind. It wrecked his resolutions. It destroyed his self-control.

Love.

He was falling in love with Mollie Parker, with her warmth and kindness and generosity of spirit, with her pansy-brown eyes and her tumble of auburn hair. With everything about her, and it terrified him.

Jacob spun away from the kitchen and the sights of his cake and his present. They were too much as well, more than he'd ever had before. He'd learned long ago not to expect presents, surprises, kindnesses of any sort. He'd trained himself not to want them.

Yet now his defences were crumbling. He felt it at night, when he fell asleep deeply enough to dream. The old nightmare came for him nearly every night now, and in it he was always worse than ever. He was a madman, a monster, and that awful laughter was his. The sound echoed endlessly through him.

Every time he woke up, sweating and shaking, he remembered the look of shock on Mollie's face when she'd seen him in the depths of that dream, and his determination to tell her the truth about himself, of what had happened and how he'd felt, to spill all his secrets, trickled coldly away.

He *couldn't.*

And yet still he wanted to. He was desperate to talk, to tell her everything in a way he had never wanted or even envisaged before. It was crazy, the way the words rose inside him, bubbled up so he could barely keep them in. Already he'd told her more than he had shared with any other person.

And she isn't walking away. She's still with you. Caring for you. Maybe even loving you...

Raking his hands through his hair, Jacob headed out into

the damp night. The grass was wet with rain and the sky black and moonless above him. He walked and breathed and tried to empty his mind of thoughts.

That old trick didn't work any more. The thoughts came anyway, memories rushing in to fill the empty spaces of his heart and mind, and the strange and surprising thing was they were *good* memories. They were memories of Mollie.

Memories of her seemed to fill the gardens and house; he could picture her bent over a plant, hard at work. Curled up on a bench in the Children's Garden, smiling wryly at being caught dozing in the sun like a contented cat. Sloshing through mud puddles in the boots he'd bought her. The memories were small, yet they still made him smile.

Made him want.

He wanted to let her know the truth. He craved the kind of exposure and honesty he'd been running from for twenty years, and yet even so, it was terrifying.

Impossible.

If he told her...

What? What would happen?

Would she reject him, if he told her just what—and who—had made him leave? Himself. The horror of his own self had forced him away from his family, before he hurt them. Before he became even more like his father.

And even more terrifying, what if he hurt Mollie? What if the old demons claimed him, and he hurt her just as he'd hurt Annabelle—or worse? That thought scared him most of all. It made his eyes darken and he turned back to his father's study, the knowledge of who he was—who he would always be—hardening inside of him.

CHAPTER TEN

THE next few days Mollie worked outside, determined to finish the renovation of the Rose Garden, although she could hardly call it that now that there were no roses in it.

She told herself she would tell Jacob she loved him, yet he'd been avoiding her again, silent and foreboding, and her courage failed her. It was so hard to say those words when you had no idea what the other person thought or felt, or whether such a declaration would even be welcome. She never found the right moment—or the courage.

The moment came when Mollie wasn't looking for it. She wasn't even ready. She was sweaty and tired from working in the garden, and came into the house for a drink of water. Yet as she stood in the kitchen, the summer sunlight slanting through the windows, she was conscious of a creeping sense of desolation; she had only one more day of work on the garden, and then there would be no excuse to stay.

She let out a long, slow breath, half wondering—half believing—that it was for the best. The weeks of Jacob's solicitous silence had started to take their toll. Maybe she loved him; maybe it didn't matter.

Sighing, Mollie gazed at the gardens in all their restored glory. She'd been so sure of her love for Jacob just a few days ago, so serene in her certainty. Yet now she felt the creeping of fear, like the most tenacious and poisonous weed, curling its destructive tendrils around her hopes. Her heart. And she didn't think she had the courage to tell Jacob anything.

She could, at least, tell him the garden was almost done. That, Mollie hoped, might give her a sense of how he felt about her leaving. Yet even that thought was nerve-racking; what if he greeted the news with calm disinterest, a careless shrug? How could she tell him she loved him *then*? How could she tell him she loved him at all?

Sighing again, Mollie went in search of Jacob in the place he spent most of his time, his father's study.

She could tell the room was empty before she even entered in. The door was ajar and a breeze blew in from the open window, ruffling the scattered papers on the desk. Mollie knew she shouldn't enter; this was Jacob's private space, his sanctum. Yet the remnant of her own memories forced her inside, to stand in the centre of the hated room and remind herself that it was just a room, in a house, and it held no power over her or even over Jacob. She could smell the clean scent of cut grass from the window, and it banished the memory of stale smoke and an excess of alcohol.

She wondered if the memories could be banished for Jacob. Coming back to Wolfe Manor had made him a slave to them, and she felt his bonds more keenly than ever. Would he ever be free? Could she help him be free?

Could her love?

A breeze ruffled the drapes once again and a few pages blew off the desk. Automatically Mollie stooped to retrieve them, and then stilled as she saw the words on the page.

Dear Annabelle. Today is your sixteenth birthday.

Mollie knew she should stop reading. These were letters, old letters, letters that had never been sent. And even though common courtesy—not to mention common sense—

told her to put these pages back on the desk unread, a deeper instinct made her keep reading.

> *I wonder what you are doing, and I hope you are able to celebrate. I hope you have cause to celebrate, for not a day goes by when I don't think of you, and pray that you are safe and loved. I left because I loved you, but I know you can't understand that now....*

Tears stung Mollie's eyes. A lump formed in her throat. She kept reading.

> *I don't expect you to understand it, or even forgive. But I want you to know that I am thinking of you, and imagining your big butterscotch cake, with sixteen pink candles to blow out. Make a wish.*

Your loving brother, Jacob

Mollie turned to the desk. A stack of papers lay on it, and she knew instinctively what they were. Letters to Jacob's family, letters he had never sent. How many had he written over the years? By the size of the stack, she guessed dozens. Maybe hundreds. She placed Annabelle's letter back on top, wanting to read the others yet knowing she had no right. Reading one letter might be forgiven, but reading them all was not.

Yet she longed to, for she knew these letters were Jacob's heart. He may have left, for whatever reason he felt so necessary, but his heart hadn't. His heart had remained with his family, and it made her love him all the more.

'What are you doing?'

Mollie froze. Jacob stood in the doorway, his face dark with suspicion and rising fury.

'Jacob,' she said weakly, and he strode into the room.

'May I help you with something?' he asked with cold politeness, and then his gaze went to his desk, and the pile of his letters. The very air in the room seemed to shiver, freeze. Jacob went utterly still, and Mollie knew he hadn't realised he'd left the letters out until that very second.

That awful second.

His gaze, dark and pitiless, swung back to her. 'Did you have a good look?' he asked, as if it was a question of nominal interest. His eyes were blacker than Mollie had ever seen.

'I—I'm sorry. The papers blew off the desk and I went to replace them.' She swallowed, knowing a full confession was required. 'I read your letter to Annabelle. I'm sorry. I know it was private, but it was beautiful, Jacob—'

'You shouldn't have.' He stalked over to the desk and swept the letters into a folder.

'Why did you never send it—them? If Annabelle could read that letter, she would—'

'She would what?' He swung around, suddenly dangerous. 'She would forgive me?'

'No, no,' Mollie said quickly. 'Just…understand. More.'

Jacob said nothing for a moment. 'Well, I've already spoken to her,' he said finally, his voice still cool. 'Several times. As a matter of fact, she's returning here next week. With her husband.'

'Her husband?' Mollie repeated incredulously.

'Yes, his name is Stefano, and she met him in Spain.' Mollie just blinked. She'd known from her friend's emails that she was doing a photography shoot in Spain, but *married*? She hadn't checked her email in ages, and she wondered if Annabelle had written her. She would have to write and offer her congratulations.

'It seems as if all of my siblings have found their happily ever after,' Jacob continued in that same cold voice. 'I've talked to them all, you know. We've made our peace with one another. If you think I'm still suffering with guilt over *that*, you're quite wrong.' Mollie opened her mouth to speak—to demand what it was that enslaved him now—but Jacob rode over her with his words. 'It's really very sweet. At least I know they'll be taken care of when I leave.'

Dread pooled in Mollie's stomach, ate away at her courage and conviction like the most corrosive acid. 'You're leaving?'

'Yes.' He met her gaze with his own bland stare. 'You always knew that, Mollie. I'm leaving, and so are you. The estate goes on the market next week. You *are* almost done the gardens, aren't you?'

She swallowed. 'Yes, but—'

'But?' Jacob prompted. He did not sound very interested.

'You could have yours too,' Mollie blurted. Desperation fuelled her words so she barely knew what she was saying. 'Your happily ever after. You could have it…with me.'

The ensuing silence, Mollie thought, was worse than anything Jacob could have said. He just stared at her until she felt like the gap-toothed, tousle-haired tomboy she'd always been, peeking through the hedges. Unseen, invisible. At least, she *wished* she was invisible now, based on the incredulous way Jacob was looking at her.

'Of course no one's happy all the time,' she continued shakily, knowing that no matter how humiliating or horrible this was, she had to see it through. 'I wouldn't expect us to be. But we could take the joys and sorrows together—sharing them…' She sounded like a greeting card. Swallowing, she tried again, in the only way she knew how. The only way left to her. 'I love you, Jacob.'

'No, you don't.' He spoke flatly, with such finality that Mollie blinked.

'Yes, I do.' Were they actually going to *argue* about it? 'Trust me, I know I do.'

Jacob let out a sharp bark of laughter that ended on a

quiet, ragged note. 'You don't love me, Mollie, because you
don't *know* me.'

'I tried to believe that,' Mollie told him. Her confidence
was growing, amazingly. She felt it come back like wind into
a sail, buoying her hope. At least he hadn't told her that he
didn't love her. Yet. 'I told myself that, because it was easier.
Safer. But I do know you, Jacob. I know what is important,
what is true—'

'No,' Jacob cut her off, his voice sharp with anger. 'You
don't.'

She took a step closer to him. She could feel the anger
and even the hurt coming off him in hot, pulsating waves.
Yet instead of scaring her, it made her sad. *Enough.* Enough
of this sorrow and heartache, this endless guilt and despair.
That time was past. She looked up at him, her eyes wide, her
face calm. 'Why don't you want me to love you, Jacob?'

'This is a pointless conversation....'

'Or is it that you're afraid I won't love you if I discover
who you truly are? This terrible secret you have?' Mollie
didn't know where she found the words; they came from a
deep place inside her, spilling out, as only truth could. She
took another step towards him and laid a hand on his arm,
as gentle as a breeze, and waited.

'I know you won't,' Jacob said in a low voice.

'Tell me.' Mollie tightened her hand on his arm. 'Tell me
why you left all those years ago. Tell me what is so terrible,
that I'm not supposed to know or understand.'

'I *can't*—'

'Why not?' Mollie challenged. 'Is it because I might
hate you? Why should that matter, if you don't love me and
you're leaving anyway? You never have to see me again.
Why should you care what I think?'

'I'm not as heartless as that,' Jacob told her quietly. The
corner of his mouth turned up in the smallest, saddest of
smiles. 'I've spent most of my life observing the people I

love from a distance. A very great distance.' He gestured to the folder still on the desk. 'I wrote those letters because I wanted to have a connection with my brothers and sister. I never posted them because I couldn't bear them to think less of me, even from far away. The memory of their love for me was what sustained me for so long.'

'And you think the memory of my love for you will sustain you?' Mollie finished. 'Why do you have to be such a martyr?' And then, to her surprise, she was suddenly angry. And she let it show. 'Tell me, Jacob, do you love me?'

He looked startled, but he didn't avoid the question. He didn't even avert his eyes. 'Yes.'

Mollie wanted to groan. Or scream. She also wanted to sing with joy. 'Then why did you just tell me you were leaving? Why can't we work through this, Jacob? Whatever it is? Isn't that what love is all about? *Trust?*'

'It's not you I don't trust,' Jacob said quietly. 'It's me.'

'You don't trust yourself?' Mollie repeated blankly. She trusted Jacob so utterly the very thought was bewildering. *'Why?'*

Jacob didn't speak for a long, tense moment. The silence ticked on, tautening the very air. The wind rustled the papers on the desk again. Mollie didn't say anything. Didn't move. She just waited.

'I remember the first time my father hit me,' he finally said, his voice quiet, calm, as if he was simply telling a story. 'I was six years old. I'd come home from school for Christmas, and I knew something was different. Wrong. Even the little ones could feel it. My stepmother, Amber, Annabelle's mother, had died—of a drug overdose, I learned later—the year before. I thought my father was sad because of that, and perhaps he was in his own way.' He took a breath and let it out slowly. 'I wanted to comfort him. I knew he wasn't like other fathers, the way dads are *supposed* to be, but as a child I kept trying to act like he was. I think I

thought if I acted that way, perhaps he would too.' He gave
her a fleeting smile, a humourless curving of his lips. 'But
of course it didn't. You can't will things into being. And
I think, looking back, that my attempts to comfort him—
to make him seem normal—frustrated him. Perhaps he realised the magnitude of his own failings.' He paused. 'That
is a hard thing to bear.' After another pause he resumed his
story. 'In any case, that Christmas he was worse than ever
before. Drunk most times, although it took me a while to realise it. It was as if...' He stopped, searching for the words
that seemed to come from the very depths of his being. 'It
was as if he'd surrendered to the worst part of himself, and
allowed it...control.'

Mollie made some inarticulate sound, as it all started to
make such terrible sense. Jacob's determination to remain
self-controlled. His refusal to drink. And he'd seen this all
when he was six.

'We had a series of temporary nannies to take care of
us, and one morning the nanny left without even telling my
father. I can hardly blame her—we were a ragtag bunch.
Jack was four and Annabelle and Alex were barely two.' He
shook his head, remembering. 'Anyway, I went in search of
my father, and found him in bed with a bottle even though
it was nearly noon. He was a mess. Weeping and raging at
turns.' Jacob's mouth twisted in memory. 'In that moment I
was so angry because I knew he should be taking care of us
and he wasn't. At least with Amber we'd had some kind of
mother. I remember her being fun and loving, at times. But
William alone...' He shook his head again. 'So I took those
whisky bottles and dumped them in the sink. I was so full
of self-righteous fury, much good it did me. My father was
unbelievably angry. I'd never seen him like that before...he
was incoherent with rage. He hit me then, and Lucas too, and
we took it because we were too young and too surprised to
know what to do. He'd never hit us before.'

'Oh, Jacob…'

'I knew then how it would be,' he finished flatly. 'How it would always be. My father may have had his good moments, when he played with us, or gave us presents, but underneath I knew what he was. So did he, and he could never escape from it. Sometimes I pitied him. Most of the time I hated him. And I always promised myself I would never, ever be like him.' He turned to face her, his expression bleak yet determined.

'You're not like him, Jacob,' Mollie whispered. 'Not one bit.'

'Yes, I am,' he returned flatly. 'I am just like him. Sometimes I hide it better, and most of the time I keep it under control. But underneath? Where it matters? We're the same.'

He spoke with such absolute conviction that Mollie wanted to cry, both for him and herself. It was hopeless. He'd never be convinced he was different, or that he was worth loving. 'I don't believe that,' she told him in a choked voice. 'I don't believe that at all.'

'You wanted to know the truth, Mollie, and now you have it.'

'This is your terrible secret?' she demanded. 'This distorted, guilt-ridden version of the past?'

'There's more…'

'Then tell me,' Mollie said, folding her arms. 'Because I want to hear it.'

'What do you want?' Jacob snarled. 'Examples? A list of all the times—'

'Yes,' she retorted. 'Yes, I would. Just when were you so like your father, Jacob? When you took care of your family? When you saved Annabelle—'

'*Saved* her?' Jacob repeated in scathing disbelief. 'I raised my hand to her.' Startled, Mollie's mouth snapped shut, and Jacob nodded as he saw her response. '*I raised my hand. I* barely kept myself from hitting her, just as my father did. She saw it. She saw my hand, and she saw the rage in my eyes, and she *cowered* from me.' He drew in a shuddering breath. 'It was after…after everything. She'd come to find me with tears in her eyes, because she needed someone to talk to. She was so lonely, shut away in the house, and so young….'

'So were you,' Mollie whispered. 'You were only eighteen, Jacob.'

'I was old enough to know better,' he returned savagely. 'Old enough to control myself.'

'You did control yourself.'

'That time.' He looked at her bleakly. 'That one time. But I knew there would be others, and who knows if I could control myself then? I didn't.' There was a new, darker note in his voice now and Mollie felt a tremble of fear ripple through her. Jacob saw it and knew what it was. He nodded. 'You're right to be afraid of me.'

'I'm not afraid of you,' Mollie returned hotly. 'No matter what you tell me now.'

'All right, then,' Jacob said. His voice was like a terrible caress, a low, silky whisper. 'Here's the truth, Mollie. Here's what you don't know. What nobody knows.' His eyes met hers, glinting blackly with challenge, and Mollie lifted her chin, ready for the worst.

'The night my father died,' Jacob told her, his voice still a soft whisper that coiled right around her heart and *squeezed*, 'I was out at a party. I liked to go out to parties. Going out and getting drunk was about the only respite I had.'

'That hardly shocks me, Jacob.'

'That's nothing,' he dismissed. 'It's what happened when I came home.'

'I know William was whipping Annabelle with a riding crop,' Mollie told him. 'She spoke of it once to me. And Nathaniel and Sebastian were trying to stop him.'

'They couldn't,' Jacob confirmed. 'They were too young. They were crying, although Annabelle was silent. She was curled up on the floor, covered in blood. I thought she was dead.'

Mollie closed her eyes. She could hardly bear to imagine the scene, and yet Jacob had lived it…and still lived with it, nearly twenty years later.

'In that moment,' Jacob told her in a cold, detached voice, 'I felt anger like I'd never known before. It was a red mist before my eyes, in my heart. It covered me. It *controlled* me, and I raised my hand to my father.'

'To save your sister,' Mollie finished swiftly. 'To save her. It was the right thing to do, Jacob. It was self-defence.'

'Was it?' he asked quietly. 'Don't you think there could have been another way? I could have grabbed the riding crop, or wrestled him to the ground, or taken Annabelle away from him.'

'Perhaps, but you could hardly consider all your choices right then,' Mollie argued. 'It was the heat of the moment.'

'Exactly. The heat of the moment. And in that heat, I wanted to hit him. So that's what I did.' He spoke with such self-loathing that Mollie felt helpless in the face of it. 'I was so angry, as angry as he'd ever been with me.'

'It's different, Jacob,' Mollie insisted. Tears crowded in her eyes and thickened her throat.

'How is it different?' His gaze suddenly swung back to her, pinning her mercilessly with its bleak truth. 'How, Mollie? I saw myself just as I really am in that moment. Someone controlled by anger, who acted on the most base instinct—'

'The instinct to protect your sister?'

'I hit him as hard as I could, Mollie. *As hard as I could.* I punched him with all the anger I'd ever felt, all the abuse I'd ever taken, and—' he drew in a shuddering breath '—in that moment, before he fell, it felt good.'

'Of course it did,' Mollie returned. 'He'd been abusing you and your brothers and sister for years, and you never fought back.' Her voice rose in an anger of her own. 'Why are you defining yourself by that one moment, instead of all the other moments when you protected your family, when you did what was right and good?'

'I have a dream,' Jacob said in a low voice. 'I dream of the moment when I hit my father—over and over again. I can't escape it. And in the dream—you heard me, didn't you? The night we were together. I laugh.' His voice shook. 'I *laugh.*'

'It's a dream, Jacob,' Mollie said steadily. 'Not the truth. Dreams distort reality, they make it worse.'

'I scared you, didn't I?' Jacob said, gazing at her bleakly. 'That night. I scare myself. I can't let go of the anger—I feel it every night, when I have that dream. And that's the truth of who I am.'

Mollie stared at him. He might laugh in a distorted dream, but now tears were running down his face, unchecked. Mollie didn't think Jacob even realised he was weeping. And without considering what she was doing, simply *needing* to, she closed the space between them and reached up to put her hands on Jacob's face, forcing him to look at her, her thumbs wiping away his tears. 'Do you know what I see when I look at you, Jacob? I see a man who sacrificed everything—even his own happiness—to protect his sister. I see a man who, time and time again, showed how much he loved his family. I see a man who has so much compassion and concern inside of him that he would do anything—*anything*—to keep from hurting the people he loves.' Jacob stared at her, unresisting, taking in every word. Mollie leaned forward, on her tiptoes, so her lips were a breath away from his. 'I see the man I love.' And then she kissed him; she could feel his shoulders shaking as she drew him towards her.

The kiss, which had started as a healing balm, turned into something hungry and urgent. Jacob's hands cupped her face and desire leapt low in Mollie's belly, scattering all the sorrow and regret.

Jacob softened his kiss, deepening it as his hands stripped away her clothes, buttons popping and scattering. Mollie fumbled with his tie, his blazer, his belt, kicking off shoes and socks and underwear until they were both naked, both breathless and desperate with longing.

Jacob drove into her in one deep stroke, filling her to completion as she pulled him even closer to her, wanting their bodies to be joined, fused from shoulder to ankle, the final healing.

'I love you,' she whispered, and he let out a choked sob. Mollie placed her hands on either side of his face, forcing him to look at her. His eyes were still full of torment, an agony she longed to wipe clean away. 'I *love* you,' she said again, forcefully, and then there were no more words as the desire became too great, spiralling dizzily inside her, higher and higher, until with a cry she found her release, and Jacob collapsed against her, his face buried in her shoulder.

He rolled away from her almost instantly, his arm thrown over his face. Mollie's heart hammered and her breath tore. She was naked and sweaty and sticky. She reached for him.

'Jacob—'

He shook his head. 'No. Don't.' He took a few ragged breaths, his chest heaving. 'You should leave me,' he said at last.

'No.' She pulled at his arm. 'I'm not leaving you, Jacob. Not now, not ever. I love you, and you love me. We're working through this.' Her voice shook and tears started in her eyes. 'We *are*.' He shook his head, a tiny movement, but Mollie felt it all the way through her. She pulled at his arm again. 'Look at me, Jacob. *Look at me*.' Finally he lowered his arm and gazed at her. In the darkness Mollie couldn't see his expression. 'I love you,' she said, her voice choked. 'I love you and I need you. Don't walk away from me. Don't think you're doing me a favour, or the right or noble thing, by leaving, because you aren't. Stay with me. Show me you love me by staying.'

Ever so gently Jacob brushed a tendril of damp hair away from her cheek. 'I'm so afraid of hurting you,' he whispered. 'More afraid of that than of anything in my life.'

A tear slipped down Mollie's cheek. 'You're a better man than you think you are, Jacob,' she whispered. 'So much better. You're a *good* man.'

Jacob gave her the faintest of smiles, yet the sight of it made Mollie want to sing or perhaps weep with relief. 'As long as you think so.'

'I do,' Mollie whispered. 'I do. You're worth saving, Jacob. Worth loving. And I love you.'

'I love you,' Jacob told her, his voice hoarse as he pulled her to him. They lay together for a long moment, neither speaking, a new peace settling over them. Yet even so, despite the relief flooding her heart that they had got this far, Mollie knew they hadn't yet made it to the other side.

The memories were still there. The sorrow and heartache and bone-deep guilt.

As long as you think so.

Yet Jacob needed to think so too. He needed to believe—in himself.

As the darkness deepened around them, Jacob stirred and finally rose from the study floor. He scooped Mollie up in his arms, smiling as she curled into him, as contented as a cat.

'I think we need a bed,' he said, and she nodded against his shoulder.

The house was swathed in darkness as he strode down the hallways to the foyer, paused at the foot of the great staircase. He'd always hated this place, hated the mental image the stairs alone conjured. Annabelle bloody. His brothers weeping. His father dead. Yet now, as he stood there for a moment, the images didn't rise up the way they usually did, and their absence gave Jacob a little flicker of hope. Perhaps the past could be forgiven. Perhaps Mollie was right.

Mollie looked up at him, her face open and so very trusting. 'Jacob?'

He smiled down at her before mounting the stairs, and she curled into him once again.

Up in his bedroom he peeled back the duvet and laid her on the bed gently, as if she might break, though he already knew how strong she was. She looked up at him, still and waiting. Jacob slid in next to her and pulled her close.

The only time he'd spent the night with a woman in the past twenty years had been the night with Mollie in the London hotel. He didn't let women close enough to see him vulnerable, to witness his sleep—or his dreams.

That night he'd been so buoyed with hope he'd risked it, with disastrous consequences. Yet now he knew there was no risk. Mollie had already seen him at his worst, at his most appalling and abject, and she loved him anyway.

She *loved* him. It felt like a miracle.

He rested his head on the softness of her hair and closed his eyes. He slept.

The dream came. Even as it attacked the fringes of his mind, Jacob felt resignation settle in his soul. He'd known this would happen. He was so agonisingly familiar with this dream; it had played in a relentless loop in his mind for too long.

Yet this time it was different. This time he wasn't in the dream; he wasn't even himself. He was a silent, invisible spectator, watching that terrible moment unfold like a scene in a play. He saw Annabelle huddled on the floor, his brothers begging their father to stop, tears in their eyes. He saw William, the riding crop raised over his head, and he saw himself.

It was strange, to look upon himself like another person, yet it also felt right. This was the truth, untainted by fear or uncertainty. He watched as his hands curled into fists; he waited, his own heart pounding, as he raised those fists. He saw his father raise the riding crop again. And then he watched himself hit his father. He heard that awful laughter.

Except it wasn't a laugh, not the laugh of his dreams, that shout of manic glee that had tormented him for so long. This was halfway to a sob, a groan of despair and anguish over what he'd just done...what he'd had to do.

And in that moment he understood himself in a way he had never had before. He understood the anger and sorrow and even that brief second of satisfaction he'd felt when he'd hit his father, and he accepted it.

He let it go.

Jacob opened his eyes, coming awake with ease and peace. Mollie was still curled close to him, asleep. His own heart rate had slowed, and he wasn't drenched in sweat as he usually was after the dream. He hadn't laughed aloud. He hadn't laughed at all.

He lay there, quietly, letting the feeling of calm acceptance spread through him. He felt different. He felt at peace. He drew Mollie close again and closed his eyes, and this time when he slept there were no dreams at all.

CHAPTER ELEVEN

MOLLIE woke to sunlight and the heavy warmth of Jacob's arm across her. She shifted, and his eyes flickered opened.

'Good morning.'

She smiled, blinking the sleep from her own eyes. 'Good morning.' She gazed at him, his features softened into a smile, and she realised she'd never seen him look so relaxed before. So at peace. 'You're different,' she said softly, and he smiled back at her.

'I feel different.' He captured her hand in his own and pressed it against her cheek. There could be no denying that this peaceful morning was a world apart from the shattered aftermath of last night's revelations. Mollie chose not to ask Jacob why. Not yet. He would tell her when he was ready.

'Come on,' she said instead. She slipped from the bed, reaching for one of Jacob's T-shirts, discarded on a nearby chair, and slipped it over her head. 'I want to show you something.'

'Show me?'

'Outside.'

Once they were both properly dressed, fortified with a quick breakfast of coffee and toast, Mollie led Jacob through the gardens. The world was bathed in fresh, lemony light, the leaves of every tree a vivid green, glittering with dew.

'You've done a marvellous job,' Jacob told her as they walked along the neat, repointed paths, the flower beds well weeded, the soil freshly turned and black. 'It's like a completely new place.'

'It is a new place,' Mollie said firmly, for what had come to her through working in the gardens—and being with Jacob—was that Wolfe Manor didn't have to suffer as a prisoner of the past, just as Jacob didn't. Just as *she* didn't.

'Where are you taking me?'

'The Rose Garden,' Mollie told him. 'Although it doesn't have roses any more.' Funny, how difficult it had been to let go of the roses. It had felt, a little bit, like letting go of her father. That garden had been so much a part of him, so dear to his heart, and yet Mollie knew he would have approved of what she'd done. Henry Parker had always believed in gardening from the heart, with both passion and purity. He would have agreed the roses had to go, even though his heart would have broken just a little bit. And she hoped—believed—he would have liked the changes she'd made. She only hoped Jacob liked them.

'Here.' She stopped at the entrance to the old Rose Garden, the hedges blocking what she'd done from Jacob's view. She stood on her tiptoes to cover his eyes. 'Don't peek.'

She felt his smile against her hand. 'Certainly not.'

Smiling back, her heart starting to beat just a bit faster, she led him to just inside the garden. 'Okay.' She took her hand from his eyes. 'Look.'

Silently Jacob surveyed the transformed space. Although the garden was still octagonal in shape, no remnant of what it had been remained. It was entirely new.

Mollie watched him take in the hand-crafted stream that marked the perimeter of the garden, and the little wooden bridge—painted red for joy—that spanned it. Slowly he walked forward, over the bridge, coming into the garden itself.

Nerves made Mollie speak, stumbling over the words. 'I—I got the idea from you, you know.'

'A Zen garden?'

'Well, yes, but not just that. At the expo I read that one of the hallmarks of J Design is how each building reflects the spirit of the owner rather than the designer. And I wanted this garden to be like that—a reflection of you.'

Jacob turned to her, startled. 'Me?'

'Yes,' Mollie said, smiling at Jacob's surprise; he looked as if he could hardly credit anything being about him. 'You're the owner of Wolfe Manor, Jacob. And you're quite an amazing person, you know.'

He caught her hand, his fingers twining with hers, and drew her to his side. 'Show me what you did.'

So Mollie did. She'd been nervous to over-explain all the choices she'd made in the garden, but with Jacob it was natural and easy to share her ideas: how she'd planted the plum trees as a symbol of resilience, since they flowered without leaf, and the pine tree as a symbol of strength. The wrought iron frog perched at a bend in the stream was a symbol of sudden enlightenment, and Jacob recognised it right away.

'"Old pond, frog jumps in, splash."' He quoted the old Japanese haiku about sudden enlightenment softly, and Mollie grinned. 'My epiphany came last night,' he told her, drawing her close again, 'thanks to you.'

He paused as they came to the main showpiece of the garden. Slightly off-centre, in a bed of raked sand, Mollie had placed eight stones. She'd chosen them carefully, from the one with glittering gold flecks that reminded her of Nathaniel's acting talent, to the smooth, grey oval whose seamless surface made her think of Annabelle's cool, collected persona. Yet the stone that drew the eye to the centre of the arrangement was the tall pillar of rough-hewn granite that presided over them all, a guardian, a gatekeeper, strong, silent, *there*. Always. She felt Jacob's hand tighten around hers as he silently counted the stones, his gaze sweeping over them and taking in the significance of the arrangement.

The stream that surrounded the garden came to its source at the top of the little rock garden, where a gradated slope turned it into a waterfall, allowing the water to spray over the rocks, bestowing them with diamond drops, before gathering in a basin below that funnelled it back to the stream bed.

Water, Mollie knew, was the symbol of rebirth, of both life and healing, and every rock was bathed by it. Jacob stretched out his hand and let the water wash over his fingers in his own silent baptism.

Then he turned to Mollie and said in a voice low with heartfelt sincerity, 'Thank you.'

They strolled through the rest of the gardens then, their hands clasped, fingers entwined, and Mollie showed him all that she had done, loving how easy it was talk to him, to point out the challenges and difficulties of each part of the project, the plants she'd worked hard to save and the ones she'd had to let go. She shook her head mournfully at the ragged stump of a huge oak tree.

'I left the stump to commemorate it,' she admitted sheepishly. 'No tree that old should just be forgotten, the stump removed like it never even was.'

'No indeed,' Jacob agreed. 'That's where we had our tree house, you know.'

'I don't remember—'

'No, my father tore it down in one of his rages.' Mollie found herself tensing slightly at the mention of William Wolfe, as if even now he held some power over Jacob, and his—their—future happiness. But Jacob just squeezed her hand and shook his head. 'It's over,' he said softly. 'I only feel sorrow now, for the man he was, and the man he could have been. The father we could have had.' He stopped, gazing at the manor, the sunlight touching its roof in gold. 'I've lived so much of my life in the shadow of what happened that night,' he said quietly. 'And not just that night, but everything that came before. Everything that led up to it.' He sighed, the sound soft, sad and accepting. 'I know I'll always regret the kind of childhood we suffered, but you've shown me that it doesn't have to cripple me. That moment doesn't have to define me.' He smiled at her, and Mollie saw that the shadows from his eyes were gone.

The night was cool and damp as Jacob rose from the bed. He left Mollie curled on her side, her hand tucked under her cheek, a smile curving her lips even in sleep. Jacob smiled at the sight of her before he pulled on a pair of drawstring trousers and a T-shirt and left the room.

He'd become accustomed to walking the manor and its grounds by night, the only respite from the hell of his nightmares. Yet tonight he'd had no dreams; he hadn't had one for nearly a week, since his ghosts had been exorcised and he'd felt the healing balm of forgiveness. He forgave himself, which seemed an incredible and amazing achievement, to seek something from within that he had not thought he'd been capable of possessing in the first place.

In the past week he'd found himself walking through the rooms of the house with a different, sweeter set of memories than he'd had before. *This is where Sebastian took his first steps. This is where Jack sledged down the back stairs on a baking tray and blacked both his eyes. This is where Lucas and I stole a batch of biscuits from Maggie and ate them until we were sick.*

He paused at the foot of the grand staircase. *This is where I saved Annabelle.*

Annabelle had rung him several weeks ago, needing his forgiveness, feeling guilty for her own sorry part in the events of that terrible night, believing herself to be responsible for driving him away. And Jacob had given it freely, without reservation or regret, for he'd never once thought she had anything to be guilty for. Yet all the while he'd held onto his own guilt, let it burn into his soul like the most corrosive acid. It was only with Mollie's help that the scars were now healing over, fading away.

He was thankful now, in a new, quiet way, for his own hand in the events of that night. It was strange, to feel gratitude after living with the soul-destroying guilt and fear for so long. Strange to let them go, and letting something cleaner and stronger take their place.

As dawn broke over the gardens, Jacob knew he had one more place to visit before the night was truly over.

Mollie woke alone. She sat up in bed, saw the first pink streaks of dawn slant through the window and illuminate the room in pale morning light, touching everything with gold. Jacob wasn't in bed; he wasn't in the room.

She slipped out of bed and quickly dressed. He was probably just working, she told herself, or perhaps just enjoying some early-morning solitude.

Yet that same fear that had been eating at her contentment all week now rose again inside of her, like a hunger that could never be satisfied. This week had been wonderful, so unbearably sweet, yet even so a pall of uncertainty hung over it. Neither she nor Jacob had talked about the future, and Mollie wondered when—or if—they would, or what kind of future they could even have. Jacob still seemed set on selling Wolfe Manor, and travelling who-knew-where.

Still, she was not about to go in search of Jacob this early in the morning and ask questions or demand answers. Instead she slipped on a pair of boots and headed out the back door, to the garden.

She left the ordered gardens behind, heading to the distant areas that had been outside her domain: the smooth, unrippled expanse of the lake, the copse of birches that was beautiful in its unexpected wildness, all the parts of the estate that were lovely without being landscaped. She loved this place, she thought with a pang of sorrow. She would be sorry to see it sold, and not just for what it might mean for her and Jacob.

She paused, coming out of the shadow of the trees, for on a hill above the woods she could see a lone figure standing in the family's private cemetery. Mollie had almost forgotten about the little graveyard on the far corner of the estate, its iron fence rusted, the gate nearly falling off its broken hinge. Her own father was buried in the local churchyard in Wolfestone. All the Wolfes, however, were buried here. Slowly she walked up the hill and slipped through the half-open gate to where Jacob was standing.

Most of the headstones in the family plot were mossy and falling down, their engraved dates worn clear away by time and weather. A few more recent headstones were in the far corner, where Jacob stood. She passed by William's wives: first Amber, then Penelope, whom she knew was Jacob's mother. She joined Jacob in front of William's grave.

Neither of them spoke. Mollie glanced at the headstone; besides the dates of William's birth and death there was a simple epitaph: *Have Mercy.*

Silently she slid her hand into Jacob's.

'It was all I could think of,' he said quietly. 'The epitaph. My father made such a mess of his life.'

Mollie said nothing. She was humbled by Jacob's selflessness, his willingness to plead for his father even while he denied himself that same mercy.

'I've been angry for so long,' he continued, his fingers tightening on hers. 'And I'm not any more. It's such a strange feeling, a lightness, not to carry that burden around. I spoke to Lucas this morning, on the telephone, and even he could tell something was different. Better.' He paused, his gaze still fixed on William's headstone. 'I only feel pity for him now. Pity and love for the man he sometimes was, the man I know he wanted to be.'

'And it's good you remember that,' Mollie told him. 'His life wasn't an utter waste, if you can hold onto that.'

The sun was breaking through the morning clouds, and the day was turning hot. Jacob turned to smile at Mollie. 'I want to show you something,' he told her. 'Something new.'

Several hours later, dressed and showered, Mollie followed Jacob out of the manor and stopped in surprise at the car parked in the drive. The little red convertible.

'You brought it back from London?'

'I had it driven.' Jacob went round to open her door. 'It's a beautiful day. We can ride with the top down.'

Mollie slipped into the car and Jacob closed the door. 'Where are we going?' she asked as they drove down the sweeping lane and then through the estate's wrought iron gates.

Jacob gave her a teasing, glinting smile. 'You'll see.'

She still wasn't prepared when, a half-hour later, they arrived at a private airstrip, a jet waiting on the tarmac. Mollie turned to him, her eyes wide. 'Jacob...?'

'Come on.' He parked and opened the door, and disbelievingly Mollie followed him towards the plane.

'A jet? But where...? I don't have anything...' She was dressed in jeans and a T-shirt, thinking he'd meant to show her something on the estate. At least she'd brushed her teeth and put on a dab of make-up, but other than that...

'I've taken care of it all,' Jacob assured her. His eyes glinted as if he knew exactly what she was thinking. 'Everything.'

Mollie gave a little laugh. This was so out of her realm, she was spinning. She decided to go with it. 'Okay,' she said, and headed up the stairs to the waiting plane.

A few minutes later the jet taxied down the airstrip and then took off into a cloudless blue sky. Across from her Jacob was grinning like a little boy with a secret. The interior of the jet was upholstered in luxurious white leather, with a mahogany coffee table between the sofas. It felt like a living room in the sky. A steward silently came forward with a bottle of sparkling cider and two flutes.

'This is amazing,' Mollie said as Jacob handed her a glass. He raised his in a toast, and she did the same.

'To amazing surprises.'

They both drank, and Mollie felt the bubbles from the cider fizz low in her belly at Jacob's heavy-lidded look. She loved everything about him, from the way his eyes glinted darkly to the low note of languor in his voice as he said, 'Come here.'

Mollie didn't pretend to misunderstand. 'Jacob, the steward—'

'He knows not to come back.'

She glanced around the little cabin, the door closed to the staff quarters on one end and the cockpit on the other. They were completely alone.

'All right,' Jacob said easily, 'if you won't come here, then I'll come to you.'

He rose from his seat with easy grace, and even after a week of exploring and learning every inch of his body Mollie's heart began to thud with expectation as he closed the space between them, sitting next to her on the sofa before pulling her onto his lap, her legs sliding across his, her breasts grazing his chest. Even now the contact felt so good, made the breath dry in her throat and the thoughts evaporate from her brain like bubbles.

Bubbles. She was filled with bubbles, light, airy, wondrous. They were miracles, really. How did they float? How did they not pop?

Jacob smiled, his hands sliding through the silk of her hair, down to her shoulders, his thumbs coming round to brush the already aching sides of her breasts.

'Jacob...' she said, but it was only a half-hearted protest as she felt the hardness of his thighs against her, and her hands

came up to flatten against the wall of his chest, then slid up
of their own accord to his shoulders, to draw him even closer
still. He was very close now, so she could smell the woodsy
tang of his aftershave and see the glint of dark stubble on his
chin. If she leaned forward just an inch she'd feel his lashes
brush her own cheek. He was still smiling faintly, and all
Mollie could think about was how much she loved him…and
how much she wanted to touch him *now*.

He dipped his head lower to hers and nipped at the corner
of her mouth, his teeth gently scraping the softness of her
lips, playful, provocative. With a groan she closed the space
between their mouths and Jacob claimed her for his own in
a deeper kiss, one hand coming up to fist in her hair and
angle her head closer to his, the other spanning her hips and
moving her so she sat straddled him, the juncture of her
thighs so achingly snug against his.

'Jacob…' she said again, breathlessly, half protest, half plea.

He smiled and reached for the zip of her jeans.

Mollie gasped at the feel of his fingers sliding against her
skin, dipping under the elastic band of her underwear. She
moved even closer so she felt the hardness of his erection
pressing into her most sensitive place, and she buried her
head in his shoulder, shifting her body as if that alone could
ease the building ache inside of her.

Jacob eased her jeans over her hips, pushing aside his
own clothing so nothing prevented their perfect joining. His
hands clasped her hips as he entered her, and his lips grazed
her jaw, nudging her to look at him. She lifted her head and
met his gaze straight on, amazed at both the pleasure and the
power of their united bodies, the deep sense of satisfaction
that was as emotional as it was physical, the feeling of com-
pleteness that overwhelmed her so she was robbed of words
or even thoughts save one.

Home. This was home.

* * *

An hour later they were in Paris. Mollie had ducked back into the bathroom to rearrange her clothing and hair, wryly noting her flushed cheeks and swollen lips. Her eyes glowed with an inner light, and she knew nothing could disguise what had just happened. She looked like a woman who had been loved.

A limousine was waiting for them as they left the airport, and within minutes they were speeding away towards the centre of the city.

'Where are we going?' Mollie asked, and Jacob just smiled. Mollie shook her head. 'All these secrets.'

'No, no secrets,' he told her. 'Just surprises.'

He took her to an exclusive hotel, and a concierge led them up to the executive suite, with its acres of plush cream carpet and a king-size bed piled high with silk pillows that Mollie knew they would put to good use.

As the concierge quietly closed the door, she spun to face Jacob, her hands on her hips. 'I'm wearing jeans.'

He just smiled, jangling the keys in his pocket. 'I told you I took care of everything.'

And he had. A few minutes later Mollie heard a knock on the door, and a young woman in a crisp white uniform told her she was ready for her spa treatments.

Instinctively Mollie glanced down at her grime-encrusted nails. She'd never even had a manicure, and for good reason. The woman glanced briefly at her workmanlike hands and smiled sweetly.

'Nothing is too much, mademoiselle. You will enjoy, you'll see.'

And she did. Three hours of manicures, massages and a plethora of other treatments left her feeling new and shiny, as if her very skin sparkled. As if she really was full of bubbles, floating down the hallway.

And then she saw the dresses.

Half a dozen haute couture gowns were laid out in the

bedroom, and Mollie almost didn't want to touch all that silk
and satin, afraid she'd get them dirty. Then she realised she
wouldn't, because she was as clean and shiny as a freshly
minted penny. She picked one and held it to her, let her
breath out in a slow hiss.

'That one is lovely,' another uniformed assistant said
crisply, bustling into the room. 'But I think the brown one
will suit your colouring better.'

'Brown?' Mollie dropped the pink satin gown she'd been
clutching. Who really wanted to wear a brown dress?

Except this dress wasn't brown at all. It was taupe, shimmering, with a ruche of cream ruffles at the daringly low
neckline, and a halter neck tied with cream silk ribbon.
When she slid the dress on, she felt nearly naked, only better.
The dress clung.

She stared at herself in the mirror, amazed at how her
curves had been accentuated. She had never even realised
she had a figure like this. She'd never worn a dress like this.

'Parfait,' the woman said, and dumbly Mollie nodded.
This whole day was *parfait*.

Next came hair, her now-lustrous waves pulled into a
sleek coil at the nape of her neck, and then make-up, finished with a dusting of shimmery powder, and finally Mollie
slid on a pair of diamond-encrusted stilettos. The assistant
handed her a matching beaded clutch and a wrap of spangled
silk in the same creamy taupe as her dress.

'Where...where's Jacob?' Mollie asked. 'Mr Wolfe?'

'He sent a car,' the assistant told her, and Mollie followed
the woman downstairs to where a limo waited in the rain-
washed Parisian night.

Within minutes she was speeding away to an unknown
destination, and when she rapped on the tinted glass that
separated her from the driver and attempted to ask where
she was going and, more importantly, where Jacob was, she
simply received a Gallic grunt in reply.

Sighing, Mollie leaned back against the leather seat and decided to simply—and literally—enjoy the ride.

A quarter of an hour later the limo pulled up to the front of a tall, modern building, elegant and spare in its lines. Mollie saw, to her surprise, that it was a museum of modern art, recently constructed. As the driver opened the door of the building, she saw a small, commemorative plaque—*J Design*—and she felt a frisson of excitement.

'Top floor, *mademoiselle*,' the driver told her, and disappeared.

The museum was deserted, although Mollie glimpsed several works of priceless art hanging on the walls. Jacob had to have some serious pulling power to be allowed into a museum without security, and she couldn't help but be impressed as she rode up in the lift and the doors whooshed open to the glassed-in penthouse, with every side open to the incredible city view.

And in the middle of all that elegant space stood Jacob.

Mollie stepped forward, taking in the table for two set with creamy linen and sparkling crystal, the two tall candles in the centre casting dancing shadows over the penthouse. She glanced around the room, and saw a few modern sculptures artfully placed.

'I feel a little overdressed,' she finally said, laughing a bit, for although Jacob looked amazing in a charcoal-grey suit, she was dressed like Cinderella about to go to the ball.

'You look beautiful.' Jacob stepped forward so the candlelight flickered over his face. 'And this is a special occasion, so you're dressed as you should be.'

'It feels very special,' Mollie admitted. She was still a little overwhelmed. She walked towards the window, gazing in amazement at the City of Light spread before her. Even though she'd never been to Paris before, she could still pick out the Eiffel Tower and the Arc de Triomphe. She felt Jacob come to stand behind her, and she leaned a little against him, revelling in his strength, and that it was hers. At least for now.

They still hadn't talked about the future, and she had a horrible, creeping suspicion that this whole surprise might be Jacob's way of saying goodbye. Go out with a bang. Or was she just being terribly insecure, because their relationship was so new and untested?

Jacob touched her lightly on the shoulders. 'I have something for you.'

'You do?' Her stomach lurched, just a little bit. She turned, smiling up at him. His eyes glinted in the candlelight.

'Yes…and it took a little doing.' He moved away from her, and when he returned seconds later he was holding something. A flower, Mollie saw. A rose.

Yet it wasn't just any rose. She could tell that as she took it and inspected the deep red centre, the orange petals a creamy white at their tips.

'It looked just as I imagined it,' Jacob said, a smile in his voice. 'Like your hair.'

'My…' Mollie gazed up at him in wonder. 'This is my father's rose.'

'The Mollie Rose,' Jacob confirmed.

She gazed down at the flame-coloured flower again, tears stinging her eyes. 'But how…?'

'A lot of favours and pulling strings.'

'I'm speechless.' She laughed a little even as she blinked back tears. 'Thank you, Jacob. This—it means a lot to me.'

'I didn't mean to make you cry,' he said softly, and touched his thumb to the corner of her eye.

'Good tears,' Mollie managed. She could still feel the imprint of his thumb on her skin.

'Then I might as well go ahead and give you all the surprises at once,' he said, and Mollie's heart bumped as he withdrew a small box of black velvet from his trouser pocket.

She could only stare, speechless, incredulous and with dawning joy, as Jacob dropped to one knee in front of her. 'Mollie Parker,' he said, his voice a low, heartfelt caress, 'will you marry me?'

CHAPTER TWELVE

'MARRY you?' Mollie repeated, as if they were words in another language, and in a way they were. In all her distant dreamings of a possible future with Jacob, she had never been so bold as to imagine this.

'Yes, marry me,' he told her, and she heard a hint of laughter in his voice at her obvious surprise. 'I'm deeply, desperately in love with you and I want you to be my wife. For ever.'

For ever. What wonderful words. 'I never thought—' Mollie began, because she really never had.

Jacob smiled. 'I didn't either,' he told her softly. 'I never thought such happiness could be mine. I never even dared to dream or hope for it. For the past nineteen years, Mollie, I've been living a half-life, or even less than that. I let myself become consumed with work because it was all I had, all that made me value myself. When I worked, I didn't remember. Didn't think. Didn't dream.' Jacob's face had become serious, his gaze still holding hers, and Mollie knew he needed to say this. She needed to hear it. 'I never let anyone close enough to find out who I really was, or at least who I thought I was, underneath.'

She reached out to touch his cheek. 'You aren't though.'

'And you made me realise that. You made me look at myself in a way I'd never been able to before. Do you know the night after I told you everything I had the old dream again? Only this time I saw it as I really was. I saw myself in a way I never had before, and I saw that I'd been tormenting myself for so long, for no purpose.' He shook his head, his lips brushing her fingers.

'Guilt has a way of getting right inside of you,' Mollie said softly, 'and keeping you captive.'

'But you set me free from it,' Jacob told her. 'Loving you has set me free, and I want to keep doing that for the rest of my life, if you let me. Will you, Mollie? Will you marry me?'

The answer was so wonderful, so easy and obvious and right. 'Yes,' Mollie said, and she held out her hand for Jacob to slip on the ring.

He held her hand gently, and she gazed in wonder at the antique diamond flanked by two perfect sapphires. 'The diamond is from my family,' Jacob explained, 'and the sapphires are new. Because we may not forget what we're from, but together we can make—and be—something better.'

'I love it,' Mollie whispered, and both laughing and crying just a little, she drew Jacob up from his knees and stepped into the loving circle of his arms.

The morning of her wedding dawned clear and bright. It had rained the night before, but now the last shreds of grey cloud were vanishing on the horizon, leaving nothing but pale blue sky.

Mollie stood at the window of her childhood bedroom; she'd decided to spend her last night as a single woman here. After they were married, the little gardener's cottage would be renovated and turned into an office space for her new landscaping business.

After Jacob had proposed, he'd told her he wanted to live in Wolfe Manor and make it a home. 'I don't want to put it on the market, and walk away from it like it never existed. Just like that big stump of yours in the garden. Wolfe Manor is my home, and it's yours too. I want to fill it with the new memories we'll make, good ones. I want to hear the laughter of our children ring through the halls, if we should be so blessed.'

Smiling, Mollie gazed out at the gardens, now touched with the gold of autumn. Staying at the manor had felt so right; she realised she couldn't imagine living anywhere else, and she was filled with joy that Jacob felt the same.

The past few months had been a whirlwind, preparing for what some magazines claimed was the 'wedding event of the year' as all the Wolfe siblings and their new spouses came back to the estate for Jacob's marriage.

Mollie had been amazed and overwhelmed to see them all together; she knew Jacob felt it too, even more than she did. Last night they'd all sat down to a catered dinner after the rehearsal, and the table had been full. The house was full. Her heart was full.

Wolfe Manor was a home again.

Mollie heard a light knock at her bedroom door and Annabelle, her matron of honour, peeked her head round the corner. 'How are you doing? I came to help you dress.'

'My stomach is full of butterflies,' Mollie admitted as she turned away from the window. 'Good ones though.'

'It's a big day,' Annabelle agreed.

'Are you feeling all right?'

Annabelle patted her slightly rounded middle and made a face. 'Fine, as long as I eat every few hours. The morning sickness is mostly gone now, but it strikes every so often.'

'Well, you look amazing,' Mollie said. She'd never seen her friend more radiant. Gone was the carefully applied layer of make-up to hide the livid red scar that cut across one cheek. Now Annabelle held her head proudly, her eyes shining with the love she had for her husband, Stefano. Gone also was the cool distance she'd cloaked herself in as a way to protect herself from the world. She smiled at Mollie and squeezed her shoulder.

'Come on, then. We'd better get moving. The photographer wants you dressed and ready to smile in an hour.'

It was going to be a big wedding. Mollie had, briefly, argued for a small, quiet affair, and Jacob would have gone along with it, but as she talked to his brothers and sister she came to accept that their older brother's wedding was the perfect event to reunite the family, as Jacob had always wanted to. How could Mollie stand in the way of that?

Now she slipped into her wedding grown, an ivory silk sheath that rippled over her skin. She wasn't the kind of girl to do ruffles or lace, and the gown made her feel sexy. Beautiful. Loved.

Annabelle twitched the gossamer veil over Mollie's bare shoulders. 'Gorgeous,' she murmured. 'Jacob is going to fall over when he sees you. Either that or grab you and head to the nearest—'

'Annabelle!' Laughing, Mollie wagged her finger at her friend. 'Actually, I think Stefano is far more likely to grab you and make a run for it. Every time he looks at you, I can see the love in his eyes. You both glow.'

'We've both been blessed, haven't we?'

'And all your brothers too.' For in the past year all the Wolfe siblings had found love, and Mollie saw the peace and happiness in each of their eyes. It was both a blessing and a bit of a miracle.

'Jacob sent this over,' Annabelle told her, reaching for a white box. 'I think it's your bouquet.' Mollie lifted the simple arrangement of flame-coloured roses from its nest of tissue paper. Annabelle made a small sound of admiration. 'I've never seen roses like that before.'

'No,' Mollie agreed quietly as she lifted the blooms to her face and inhaled their heady scent, 'you wouldn't have.'

Jacob shifted from foot to foot as he stood at the front of several dozen rows of white folding chairs set out on the estate's

grand lawn. He still wasn't used to being the centre of attention, the focus of so many pairs of eyes. He wanted Mollie
to make an appearance just so people would stop looking at
him so much.

He also wanted to see her. Touch her. Hold her in his arms
and promise to make her his for ever. The thought, even now,
had the power to bring him to his knees, so utterly thankful
for the mercy that had been shown him.

From his position beside Jacob, Lucas murmured out of
the corner of his mouth, 'Don't break down yet. She hasn't
even made an appearance.'

Jacob gave his best man a rather crooked smile. He knew
Lucas understood how big a day this was. All of his brothers knew, and his sister as well; they were all married. All in
love. All happy.

It was more, so much more, than he'd ever dared to dream
of. Hope for. He straightened as the other groomsmen—
Alex, Jack, Nathaniel, Sebastian, Rafael and Annabelle's
husband, Stefano—joined him at the front, radiating out
from his side.

The minister gave a tiny cough, and Jacob jerked his
gaze to the back of the rows of chairs. The first bridesmaid,
Aneesa, Sebastian's wife, was coming down the aisle, wad-
dling a little as her first baby was due any day now.

Jacob's gaze followed each lovely woman as she came
down the aisle, smiling with the joy of the upcoming cere-
mony and the serenity of knowing she already had that happiness and love for herself. After Aneesa, came Alex's wife,
Libby, and then Nathaniel's wife, Katie, now six months
pregnant and utterly radiant. Jack's wife, Cara, followed, and
then Grace, Lucas's wife. Rafael's gorgeous wife, Leila, also
very heavily pregnant with their precious twin babies, came
next—somewhat slowly—and lastly Annabelle, smiling, her
scar barely noticeable.

And then Mollie. Gorgeous, loving, wonderful Mollie.

Jacob could see the sparkle in her pansy-brown eyes from the front, felt the love radiating out from her in warm, giving rays. His face broke into the widest, most ridiculous grin.

He was so *happy*.

And as Mollie joined his side, her smile matching his own, the minister gave another little cough and said, 'Shall we begin?'

Two hours later Jacob was tired of smiling, yet somehow he still couldn't stop. They'd been taking photographs for hours, and even though they'd already agreed on the deal to sell the snaps to a celebrity magazine for a huge sum, all of which would go to a charity for the prevention of child abuse, he was ready to be done with it. He wanted to eat. He wanted to dance. He wanted to go upstairs and make love to his wife.

'You're looking a little hot under the collar,' Jack remarked as he came to stand beside Jacob. Jacob smiled wryly.

'Just a bit tired of the photos.' He glanced sideways at Jack, knowing that the rift that had grown between them had not yet truly healed. He hadn't had a chance to speak privately with his brother, not since Jack had accused him of running away a second time by selling Wolfe Manor. He glanced up at the stately house he would always know as home. He was finished with running away. 'Jack, I know the last time we spoke—'

Jack shook his head. 'I was angry….'

'You had good reason,' Jacob said quietly. 'I'll never take lightly how much I hurt you all by leaving.'

'It's finished, Jacob.'

'I know it is.' And he did, deep within.

Jack gave him a crooked smile. 'Look at us all now. We've made it through all right, I'd say.'

'Thanks to some amazing women,' Jacob half joked, although his eyes were on Mollie.

'And one amazing man. I've never seen Annabelle look so beautiful.' Jack clapped his brother on the shoulder. 'The past really is finished.'

Jacob nodded and pulled his brother into a quick, fierce hug before letting him go and nodding towards Mollie. 'And now it's time I claim my bride.'

Jacob pulled Mollie away from the circle of guests, leading towards the sheltered privacy of the gardens.

'Where are you taking me?' she asked, laughing a little. 'Our guests, Jacob—'

'I'm taking you away,' he told her. 'Somewhere. Anywhere. I just want to be alone with you.'

Under an oak tree, in a pool of dappled sunlight, he drew her into his arms and kissed her thoroughly—although not as thoroughly as he wanted to, or as he certainly would later.

Mollie tipped her head up, smiling into his eyes. 'This kind of happiness almost doesn't feel real. Like a dream.'

'Not a dream,' he assured her, tucking a stray tendril of hair behind her ear. 'No more dreams, no more regrets, no more looking back.' He kissed her again, filled with a deep sense of peace, overwhelmed with a lasting, buoyant happiness. 'This is real. This is our future, Mrs Wolfe.'

* * * * *

CLASSIC

Quintessential, modern love stories
that are romance at its finest.

You can find more information on upcoming Harlequin® titles,
free excerpts and more at www.HarlequinInsideRomance.com.

HPCNM0212

REQUEST YOUR FREE BOOKS!

◆Harlequin *Presents*®

PASSION GUARANTEED SEDUCTION

2 FREE NOVELS PLUS
2 FREE GIFTS!

YES! Please send me 2 FREE Harlequin Presents® novels and my 2 FREE gifts (gifts are worth about $10). After receiving them, if I don't wish to receive any more books, I can return the shipping statement marked "cancel." If I don't cancel, I will receive 6 brand-new novels every month and be billed just $4.30 per book in the U.S. or $4.99 per book in Canada. That's a saving of at least 14% off the cover price! It's quite a bargain! Shipping and handling is just 50¢ per book in the U.S. and 75¢ per book in Canada.* I understand that accepting the 2 free books and gifts places me under no obligation to buy anything. I can always return a shipment and cancel at any time. Even if I never buy another book, the two free books and gifts are mine to keep forever.   106/306 HDN FERQ

Name	(PLEASE PRINT)

Address	Apt. #

City	State/Prov.	Zip/Postal Code

Signature (if under 18, a parent or guardian must sign)

Mail to the **Reader Service:**
IN U.S.A.: P.O. Box 1867, Buffalo, NY 14240-1867
IN CANADA: P.O. Box 609, Fort Erie, Ontario L2A 5X3

Not valid for current subscribers to Harlequin Presents books.

**Are you a current subscriber to Harlequin Presents books
and want to receive the larger-print edition?
Call 1-800-873-8635 or visit www.ReaderService.com.**

* Terms and prices subject to change without notice. Prices do not include applicable taxes. Sales tax applicable in N.Y. Canadian residents will be charged applicable taxes. Offer not valid in Quebec. This offer is limited to one order per household. All orders subject to credit approval. Credit or debit balances in a customer's account(s) may be offset by any other outstanding balance owed by or to the customer. Please allow 4 to 6 weeks for delivery. Offer available while quantities last.

Your Privacy—The Reader Service is committed to protecting your privacy. Our Privacy Policy is available online at www.ReaderService.com or upon request from the Reader Service.

We make a portion of our mailing list available to reputable third parties that offer products we believe may interest you. If you prefer that we not exchange your name with third parties, or if you wish to clarify or modify your communication preferences, please visit us at www.ReaderService.com/consumerschoice or write to us at Reader Service Preference Service, P.O. Box 9062, Buffalo, NY 14269. Include your complete name and address.

HP11B

New York Times *and* USA TODAY *bestselling author*
Maya Banks presents book three in her miniseries
PREGNANCY & PASSION.

TEMPTED BY HER INNOCENT KISS

Available March 2012 from Harlequin Desire!

There came a time in a man's life when he knew he was well and truly caught. Devon Carter stared down at the diamond ring nestled in velvet and acknowledged that this was one such time. He snapped the lid closed and shoved the box into the breast pocket of his suit.

He had two choices. He could marry Ashley Copeland and fulfill his goal of merging his company with Copeland Hotels, thus creating the largest, most exclusive line of resorts in the world, or he could refuse and lose it all.

Put in that light, there wasn't much he could do except pop the question.

The doorman to his Manhattan high-rise apartment hurried to open the door as Devon strode toward the street. He took a deep breath before ducking into his car, and the driver pulled into traffic.

Tonight was the night. All of his careful wooing, the countless dinners, kisses that started brief and casual and became more breathless—all a lead-up to tonight. Tonight his seduction of Ashley Copeland would be complete, and then he'd ask her to marry him.

He shook his head as the absurdity of the situation hit him for the hundredth time. Personally, he thought William Copeland was crazy for forcing his daughter down Devon's throat.

Ashley was a sweet enough girl, but Devon had no desire

to marry anyone.

William had other plans. He'd told Devon that Ashley had no head for the family business. She was too softhearted, too naive. So he'd made Ashley part of the deal. The catch? Ashley wasn't to know of it. Which meant Devon was stuck playing stupid games.

Ashley was supposed to think this was a grand love match. She was a starry-eyed woman who preferred her animal-rescue foundation over board meetings, charts and financials for Copeland Hotels.

If she ever found out the truth, she wouldn't take it well.

And hell, he couldn't blame her.

But no matter the reason for his proposal, before the night was over, she'd have no doubts that she belonged to him.

What will happen when Devon marries Ashley?
Find out in Maya Banks's passionate new novel
TEMPTED BY HER INNOCENT KISS
Available March 2012 from Harlequin Desire!